Look to the Hills

The Diary of Lozette Moreau, a French Slave Girl

BY PATRICIA C. MCKISSACK

Scholastic Inc. New York

Aix-en-Provence, France
1763

(The first part of Lozette Moreau's diary was written in French. It was translated for this publication.)

Aix-en-Provence, France
Tuesday, January 4, 1763

My name is Lozette Moreau, even though everybody calls me Zettie. I found this small memory book in a box cast away in the corner of my tiny room, very much the way I have been discarded. No more than a thing. I have no idea of what the future holds for me, but I have decided to record the events day by day.

I begin by saying I am a companion. That is just a fancy word for slave. My duty is to be a companion to Marie-Louise Boyer. Her father, André Defoe Marquis de Boyer, purchased me for that single purpose. Being her companion is what I have always done. But now, my life is about to change drastically. The Boyer family has been driven into financial ruin by the marquis's heir, Pierre Boyer. Because of Pierre Boyer's reckless schemes and mismanagement, creditors are going to sell off everything on the fifteenth of the month to satisfy his debts. That everything includes me.

I've always known I was a slave. But knowing it was like knowing that it is Monday or August or summer. I am like so many girls who serve as companions to the daughters of aristocrats. We grow up with our mistresses, catering to their every wish. We go wherever they go. See what they see. Hear what they hear. Learn what they learn. We are trained to be loyal and honest, well mannered and poised. For good service we are usually freed when our young mistress gets married.

I never worried much about my condition, because it did not occur to me that I was "property." Besides, I believed that the marquis was going to free me when Marie-Louise married. Now he is dead, and a dead man cannot set me free.

Foolishly I believed that the house on Argonne Street in the heart of Aix-en-Provence was always going to be my home.

But now I know better. Living in a large house does not make me free.

I am still a slave.

Sharing secrets with Marie-Louise does not make me a family member.

I am still a slave.

Speaking fluent French does not make me a citizen of France.

I am a slave. And saying it is like vomiting up rotten meat.

Afternoon

Pierre is keeping me locked in this dreadful little room on the top floor of the maison Boyer to make sure I do not run away. It is hot and dusty, cluttered with old clothing, toys, and furniture. And all there is to sleep on is a pallet made of coverlets. I have never slept on the floor in my life! I slept in my own bed in a small alcove of Ree's room. Ree is my special name for Marie-Louise. I have always called her that, and she has always called me Zettie.

Wednesday, January 5, 1763

Pierre has forbidden Ree to come to my room. And, of course, Ree ignored her brother, as she always does. I was so glad.

"Am I really going to be sold?" I asked. I've never been so frightened.

"Hush, hush, my pet," she said lovingly. She smoothed my eyebrows the way she has done as long as I can remember. "Haven't I always taken good care of you?"

I nodded my head and fought back the tears. "You are really upset, my little Zettie," she said, somewhat surprised. "Look at you. Why, you never show any fear with a fencing sword in your hand, facing an opponent twice your size. Yet, you are in tears because of the likes of Pierre."

I do not know where I got the courage to ask, but I did. "Why can't you free me?"

"It is complicated," she answered. "Pappa owned you, even though he gave you to me. When he died, all his property — including you — legally was his. So, my hands are tied."

I was desperate. One of the other companions betrayed the trust of her mistress, and she was sold to a plantation in the West Indies. She didn't last a year. I'm so afraid I'll be sent there. "Why don't you buy me?" I pleaded. But it was a useless cry. Ree lives in luxury, but she has no money of her own.

"Would you free me if you could?" Somehow her answer was important to me.

"I would free you if I was sure you could take care

of yourself." She thought for a moment. "Perhaps at my age — eighteen." Six whole years!

Ree told me not to worry and promised that everything was going to be set straight. But she didn't tell me how.

Thursday, January 6, 1763

Ree came to see me again today. "Oh, Zettie!" she said, fury twisting her face. "Pierre has promised me in marriage to Jean-Paul Beloit, the banker."

"The Toad Banker!" I was shocked. Ree and I often made light of Jean-Paul, whose pear-shaped body makes him look like an ugly toad. He has beady black eyes, set far apart. His wig is never on straight, and his breath reeks of garlic. Marry him? Never!

Although Ree is eighteen and most women her age are married, she is not like other women. She never has been one to seek the company of men in a romantic way. She would rather challenge one to a duel.

Marie-Louise Boyer is one of the best duelists in France — male or female. She took up the sport because her father was the fencing instructor of the king's guards and a champion in his own right. Ree has dueled with some of the best swordsmen in France, including Saint Georges. Whenever Saint Georges is in Provence, he stops by to practice with Ree.

The first time I ever saw Saint Georges was when he came to winter with his adopted family in Provence a few years ago. He visited with the marquis with the hopes of getting a few pointers on his style and technique. I had heard the rumors about him. That he is a mulatto, which means his father is French and his mother is African. And that he is a brilliant swordsman, archer, horseman, and poet. But when I saw him it was just as I imagined the Archangel Gabriel might look — tall and straight as an arrow. He had tight curly hair and olive-colored skin.

Saint Georges is the only person I ever saw disarm the marquis in a single move. After one duel, the marquis announced that though Saint Georges was only sixteen, he was already a master.

I am not as skilled at fencing as either he or Ree, but I am a good study. He is in town. It would be nice to see him before I am . . . sold.

"Are you listening to me?" Ree asked, bringing me out of my daydreams about Saint Georges.

"The Toad is old enough to be your father," I answered quickly. "Is Pierre that desperate?"

Ree buried her face in her hands. "Pierre will agree to do anything to stay out of debtor's prison — including using me to secure a loan from Jean-Paul."

"None of this would be happening if your older brother were still alive," I said.

"Jacques is dead. Father is dead. I will get us out of this somehow. Don't worry."

I hope so.

Friday, January 7, 1763

All of the Boyer slaves have been sold, except me, and the free servants have been let go. Callie the cook and Charles the gardener were sold this morning. From the window I saw them led away. I will miss Callie's shrill voice, snapping demands for us to clear out of her kitchen. And who will talk to the beautiful roses and coax them into bloom now that Charles is gone? I pressed my face against the window to get one more look at two dear people I will probably never see again. Pierre didn't allow me to say good-bye.

Saturday, January 8, 1763

Belle warned me that this day might come. Too bad I didn't listen to her. She was the Boyers' nursemaid who took care of both the Boyer sons. When Madame Boyer died, Belle finished raising Ree and trained me to be Ree's companion. She had served Madame Boyer since they were both ten years old. After years of loyal service, the marquis freed her shortly after his wife died. Pierre fired her last year for insubordination! What a foolish man.

Belle was blunt, but she was a kind person deep inside, where it counts. Belle was the first person who ever spoke to me about freedom.

Ree was eight years old when the marquis brought me to the house as a gift for his daughter. From that day, I went everywhere with her. I was content to be a companion.

One day, Belle gave me a warning. "Never forget — not for one second — that you are a slave, Zettie. You will move within Marie-Louise's circle of privilege, but you, yourself, are not privileged." At first I didn't understand. She was attacking the only life I had ever known.

"But I am a loved and trusted — "

"What, companion?" she interrupted. "That is a pretty word that flatters a fool. You are a slave. Owned like a puppy dog. You come when you are called. You stay where you are told. You eat what you are given. You leave when you are told to leave. You have no say in your life."

I scoffed. Belle was just envious of the freedom I enjoyed. When I accused her of being jealous, Belle looked at me squarely in the face. "You are confused, child," she said. "You are not better off than a working slave because you accompany your mistress to a concert or a party. As long as you keep your eyes cast down at your feet you will remain no more than an eager mutt, with no mind of your own. You must lift your head and look to the hills."

"Why look to the hills?" I asked.

"Looking will make you curious about what's on the other side of them. And sooner or later you will be compelled to go see freedom."

The last thing Belle said to me before leaving was, "Always look to the hills, Zettie."

Lately I've been thinking about Belle, and I want to see what's on the other side of those hills. Is freedom really there?

Later

The marquis used to quote the philosopher René Descartes: *Cogito, ergo sum.* Which means: I think, therefore I am.

I am, too. I speak. I think. I write. I feel. I cry. I have laughed. I still dream. Yet, on the fifteenth, I will go to the highest bidder as a thing — the same as the Boyer family's olive groves outside Marseilles, the imported Spanish table in the hallway, the chaise covered in silk brocade, the handmade chest, and the ornate brass bed.

There! In the moonlight I just saw a man leap over the wall. I cross myself for fear it might be a demon on the prowl. I'd better put out the light.

Sunday, January 9, 1763

Saint Georges came to the house today. Ree was glad to see him, and so was I. He was his usual, handsome self. Colorful and stylish.

"Word of your troubles has come to my attention, and I came to offer my services in any way that I might be needed," he said, bowing graciously.

Pierre doesn't like Saint Georges. It is so obvious.

Pierre found some excuse to leave, but he was careful not to insult Saint Georges. Pierre is a decent swordsman, but he is no match for Saint Georges — or his sister, for that matter.

Saint Georges expressed his best wishes and sorrow that I am to be sold. "I would buy you and free you all in the same day, Zettie. But I have no money of my own, yet."

It made me feel special that Saint Georges is concerned about my well-being. Most mulattos care little for a slave and distance themselves, hoping they will not be confused for one of us. But not Saint Georges.

After a good practice with foils, during which Ree was very aggressive, Saint Georges emerged the victor. He saluted us with his sword, then departed. The thought of never seeing him again nearly breaks my heart.

Monday, January 10, 1763

The appraisers came today. Pierre brought me to the great room and stood me beside the window, where the light was on my face. I felt like an object, not a person. Marie-Louise looked on, showing no emotion in her face. I would not look at her, lest I cry. I was too stunned to move.

"Pure African stock?" one of the men asked, squeezing me on the arms and shoulders the way one feels melons in the marketplace.

"Both parents African. She will bring a good price in the West Indies," said the tall, thin appraiser, who held my chin in his hand and snatched my face from side to side as if examining a horse.

"She's been a companion all her life, so she won't last in the fields. But she speaks upper-class French, and she's fluent in English and Spanish as well," said the other man.

The first bank appraiser chuckled. "All that refinement isn't worth two dead flies on a sugarcane plantation. But to some gentleman needing a companion for his daughter, she might be priceless."

I have never been so humiliated in my life. All I can do is lie on my pallet and beg for sleep to come.

Later

Tonight I heard scratching outside my window. I looked, but saw nothing. Then moments later I heard voices on the balcony below me. My door was locked, so I was unable to get out to investigate further. Has the shadowy figure I saw the other night come back? Who could it be? For what purpose? These are strange times.

Tuesday, January 11, 1763

Pierre told me to pack what few things I could call my own. But he also warned me not to take a thread that didn't belong to me, otherwise I will be carted off to the dreadful prison, the Château d'If. It is he who should be worried about being sent there for the debts that he is unable to pay.

In a way, my birth and his birth put us at odds with each other. Pierre was born the second son of the marquis. He has lived in the lap of comfort and ease. For me, life began differently.

Nearly thirteen years ago, my blessed mother was captured and taken from her home on Africa's shore. On the ninth day of December, she died after giving birth to me onboard the slave ship *Angeline*, docked outside the port at Marseilles, France. I became the property of the ship's captain, Bruchard Moreau. The captain wrapped me in the cloth that my mother was covered in. That is all I have of her.

Then, taking care of his investment, the captain had me baptized, named me Lozette, and tacked on his last name, Moreau.

Captain Moreau placed me with the nuns at the Convent of Ste. Genevieve. For a year and six months, they took care of me. When the captain returned to claim his property, the sisters protested, but the law was on his side.

As fate would have it, Captain Moreau sold me to the Marquis de Boyer, a wealthy widower who wanted a companion to console his daughter, Ree, who had just lost her mother in an epidemic. That is how I came to live here in the Boyer household with Ree, Jacques, and Pierre, and twenty-one other slaves and servants.

Ree never treated me like a slave, and Pierre resented it. He accused his sister of being too liberal.

"Pappa, may I remind you that Lozette is a slave!" Pierre hissed on the "s" sound like a reptile. He was outraged because I called Marie-Louise and Jacques by their given names, without including a title. "It is silly," said Ree, "for Zettie to call me Mademoiselle and Marie and Louise when Ree works perfectly well." Jacques didn't care, either. He was always busy fixing the wing of a broken bird, or putting a bandage on one of the household pets.

But Pierre insisted that I call him Monsieur Pierre. "Mama always said I should not allow a slave to become too familiar with me or other members of the family."

I held my breath waiting for the marquis's answer. He was a man of honor, fair in all affairs, kind to a flaw, and strong and forceful when he needed to be. His reply that day was to the point: "It is you, my son, who should be careful about becoming too familiar with me about matters that don't concern you. Zettie makes Ree happy. That makes me happy."

"Understood," replied Pierre, bowing his head respectfully. Pierre carefully put his feelings in a secret bag and let them fester like a sore. Oh, to keep the peace, I called him Monsieur Pierre in public. Pierre behind his back. And in front of others he treated me much the way the rest of the family did. I was arrogant — too foolish to realize how defenseless I would be when my protector was gone. It is now Pierre's hour.

Later

There was whispering on the balcony again tonight. I strained to hear what was being said. Nothing. One of the voices was female. Ree? She is the only female in the house other than me. Since I am not on the roof, then it must be she.

Why is Ree up there, and with whom?

Wednesday, January 12, 1763

Ree came to my room, but this time Pierre followed her. He accused us of plotting against him and locked me inside the room. I know that Ree has always been able to handle her brothers. She will again.

The brothers. They are six and seven years older than Ree. Jacques was as loving as Pierre was nasty. They are only a year apart in age, but centuries apart in spirit. Jacques was the oldest. Wise. Brave. Good. Honest. A real gentleman.

It feels like yesterday that Jacques came home from the university, where he was studying medicine, to announce that he had joined the army to defend France in yet another war with England. The fighting this time has been going on for almost seven years — a costly war in time and money. It has dragged on for as long as I can remember. The marquis was so proud of his son. While other nobles' sons were paying people to serve in their places, Jacques joined the military freely.

Young Lieutenant Jacques Boyer was sent to New France in North America. The marquis read all of Jacques's letters to the complete household. Of course, Pierre never came to a reading. He thought it was inappropriate.

Jacques mentioned the servants by name, asking about our well-being. It brought tears to our eyes each time a letter came. He always spoke lovingly to his sister, wishing her all good things, joy, peace, and happiness. "Try not to intimidate the suitors who must be clamoring at the door," he wrote to her.

Jacques kept us informed about the war with England, the various battles, the generals, and the gallantry of his fellow French soldiers. Some Indians fought with the French and some, called the Iroquois, fought with the English. He talked about the colonial militias and how they fought to protect and defend their farms and homes in New France.

What I remember most about Jacques's letters are his descriptions of Fort Niagara and the Great Falls called by the same name. He drew pictures of the animals he saw and the Indians he encountered — a Huron warrior, a Miami child. He wrote words that helped me see the mountains, the crystal-clear streams, the morning mists among the trees. It sounded so different from Provence. Wild. Frightening. Fascinating.

The last time we heard from Jacques, he was at Fort Pontchartrain du Detroit.

"The war does not go well for the French," he wrote in his last letter to his father, received in late 1759. "Louis-Joseph, Marquis de Montcalm is a military genius and one of the bravest men I know," he continued. "It has been a privilege to serve under him, but we are in need of supplies and support. We have lost Fort Duquesne, Fort Niagara, the fortress at Louisbourg, and Quebec is under siege. . . ."

We heard nothing from him until a letter arrived in May 1761 from his commanding officer, stating that Lieutenant Jacques Boyer had been killed defending Fort Pontchartrain du Detroit against the British, on November 10, 1760. The entire household mourned.

The marquis was so upset by the news of his son's death, he was stricken with a paralysis from which he never recovered. Within a week he was buried in the Cathédrale de Saint-Sauveur.

Being the only surviving son, Pierre inherited his father's titles, money, and lands. It would have been better to toss it to the wind. Pierre has the business sense of a flea and the moral backbone of an eel. So it didn't take long for him to lose everything it took his family generations to build, including the olive oil plantations near Marseille.

Later

The Toad came to see Ree tonight. I saw his carriage from the window. I am worried.

Whenever I am deeply troubled, I wrap myself in my mother's cloth. I bury my face in the folds and try to smell her image into my head. It comforts me.

I closed my eyes and tried to imagine what my mother looked like. Are my almond-shaped eyes her eyes? Are my wide nose and high cheekbones those of my father? Maybe one day I will be free. Then I will go beyond the mountains into Africa and look for my people.

Thursday, January 13, 1763

Ree begged Pierre to allow me to go downstairs to practice dueling with her in the courtyard. He warned us that if we tried something — anything — he would lock us both away. "Nothing must go wrong on Saturday."

I was at last able to ask Ree about the shadow person I had seen and heard for several nights. But she insisted upon speaking first. She seemed more cheerful than usual. Her cheeks were rosy, and her eyes held the light, which made them sparkle. I knew her better than most, and if I had not known better, I would have thought she was happy.

"I have wonderful news, Zettie," she said.

"News? Tell me quickly or I will burst with anticipation."

"Look!" she squealed, and held out her arm. On it was a bracelet with many colorful jewels hanging from golden hoops. She twisted her arm, and the baubles jangled. "It's a gift from Monsieur Jean-Paul," she said, her eyes fluttering.

"The Toad?" She had accepted jewelry from that awful man and was happy about it?

"Oh, Zettie, shush! He is a wonderful person once

you get to know him," she said, gushing praise. "He's kind, and considerate, and — "

"And he's a toad," I whispered in disbelief.

"Zettie, that will be enough! You forget yourself. You can't speak to me that way. We are not equals." Her words cut across my spirit like a jagged knife. She rushed on, saying, "Jean-Paul wants to get married right away. I am no longer resisting the inevitable. I have my future to look after now. You would do well to do the same, Zettie."

I hardly heard a word. I tried to see some hint of a practical joke, but there was nothing. Ree was serious. She turned her back on me, saying, "I asked Monsieur Beloit to purchase you for me as a wedding gift. And he has graciously agreed. I assured him that you could be retrained to be an excellent cook and laundress. Isn't that nice?"

Anger seized me, and I blurted out, "No! It is a horrible idea."

Pierre, who had been eavesdropping on the conversation, stormed out of the house and slapped me across the face. I had never been struck in anger before. "See, I told you," he said. "She needs discipline!" He raised his hand to strike me again.

"No," shouted Ree. "You are right. I have let her get

away with far too much. But I know better now. I will discipline Zettie myself."

This seemed to satisfy Pierre. He lowered his hand. Then he nodded his approval with Ree. Sneering at me, he went back into the house.

"Oh, Zettie," she said, hugging me up close. "Whatever I do, it is for your good."

I held my hurt inside. Pulling away, I asked as politely as I could manage to be excused, even addressing her as Mademoiselle Marie-Louise. Once out of her sight, I burst into tears.

My eyes are dry now.

Looking out the tiny window of this room, I lifted my head and gazed over the rooftops to the blue hills that tower in the distance. I remember Belle's words. And I make a vow: One day, I will see what's on the other side and be free.

Saturday, January 15, 1763

I write in haste. I don't know when I will be able to write again or where I will be when I do. I was sold today like a basket of grapes. The Toad purchased me, while Ree clung to his arm squealing with delight. One of the appraisers opened the bidding at 20 francs, but quickly the Toad jumped the bid to 30 francs. There were a few more exchanges until the total reached 70 francs.

"Hurry and get your things, Zettie. Monsieur Beloit has arranged for us to leave immediately for Paris. The carriage is waiting," Ree shouted, impatiently.

Everything in the house has been sold, even the grand house itself. It is the only home I have ever known. Leaving it is like being ripped from a loved one. Suddenly, I am flooded with memories of earlier times, when laughter and music filled the rooms.

Ree calls. My things are packed. I check to make sure I have my mother's cloth. Time to go. God only knows where.

Two Weeks Later . . .
Friday, January 28, 1763

I am in Cádiz, Spain.

How did I get here? It is a miracle. My head is still spinning from the events. Although it is late and my body is tired, I want to write everything down before I forget.

After being sold, I was loaded into the carriage

along with the Toad, Ree, and Pierre, bound for the new house Jean-Paul had purchased outside of Paris. We had scarcely reached the city limits of Aix-en-Provence when the coachman came to a halt.

"What is the matter?" Pierre yelled impatiently out the window. Suddenly the door was snatched open and two hooded bandits ordered the men out of the carriage at sword point. One used a false tone to his voice, a high-pitched, silly voice.

"Here, take all the money I have," said Jean-Paul. "Just don't hurt me."

Pierre looked disgusted. Pulling his sword, he challenged one of the bandits, who was clearly the more superior swordsman. With a quick thrust, the bandit took Pierre by surprise. He lost his balance, but before falling, he tossed his sword to Ree. "Finish him!"

Ree engaged the bandit, but I could see she wasn't really making an effort to defend herself. Why? Within seconds she made a lunge wildly and was put on the defensive. Another move and she was disarmed. I couldn't believe it!

"A noble gesture," said the bandit in a fake shrill voice. Then he pulled Ree inside the carriage and tied her hands with a rope. Then he turned to me. I kicked and screamed and tried to free myself.

"Hold still. I'm trying to help you," my captor whispered in his natural voice. My body went limp because I recognized who it was. The other bandit hopped into the driver's seat and took the reins of the carriage.

Jean-Paul, Pierre, and the coachman were told to strip down to their underwear and to remove their boots. With a flick of the whip, we sped away, leaving Pierre and Jean-Paul behind to make their way back to town.

When we were well out of sight, we all burst into laughter. The bandit removed his hood, and it was Saint Georges!

We laughed for miles, remembering the sight of the Toad and Pierre standing in the middle of the road in their underwear. The Toad's wig was on lopsided. That made me laugh even harder.

"It was you I saw in the courtyard and heard on the roof talking to Ree," I said to Saint Georges. "You were planning this all along?"

"I simply came to the aid of two friends as soon as I heard what was happening," he said, smiling. "But, it was Ree who was the mastermind of the whole escape."

"Zettie, I was unkind to you, I know," said Ree. "But I had to make Pierre think I had changed."

I was happy that we were escaping, I didn't care about what I had endured. If I had to be a slave, then I would rather be owned by Ree than anyone else.

The carriage sped south. I still didn't know where we were going or how we would get there, but I was happy to be on my way.

Later the Same Day

Before leaving us at the port of Marseilles, Saint Georges told us about a friend of his who had been captured by the Delaware Indians in the Americas. The friend had escaped and made his way back to France. "The soldier told me that he was held in captivity with Jacques. He is living among the Indians. And refused to escape when he could."

"But that's impossible," said Ree. "He was killed at Fort Pontchartrain du Detroit."

"It seems he wasn't," answered Saint Georges.

"Is he well? Is he being mistreated? What?"

Saint Georges knew nothing more, but he did tell Ree that the officer who escaped is going to make a full report on Jacques's whereabouts and his refusal to escape when he could.

Ree has changed all previous plans. She's going to

the Americas to search for her brother. "If he is alive, then I must find him and bring him home."

How on earth does she intend to do that? She has no money.

More . . .

With the help of family friends, Ree has arranged passage for us on a ship to Cádiz, Spain. Her godfather, Señor Orlando Ortega, lives there.

Saying our farewells to Saint Georges on the dock was difficult. I didn't know what to say. Suddenly he picked me up and swung me around. "One day, Lozette Moreau, I'm going to find you wherever you are on this earth and marry you."

I knew he was joking. He didn't mean it . . . I don't think. It would be wonderful if he did, but . . . "I don't believe you," I said.

Saint Georges laughed. "You know me too well," he said. Then, with another round of hugs and a dramatic swish of his cape, he was gone.

Once we reached Señor Ortega's house, he and his wife made Marie-Louise welcome. "Stay with us here, as long as you wish," he said.

Getting straight to the point, Ree told him about

Jacques and how she needed to get to New France in the North American colonies to search for him. "He is still alive," she said.

"How do you know for sure?" Señor Ortega asked. "My nephew Juan and his wife manage my trading store at Fort Louisbourg on the island of Cape Breton." Señor Ortega continued: "Let me have them seek out the truth before you go off into that great wilderness."

That made good sense to me. But Ree would not listen. She insisted that her brother's well-being was a matter of honor. She had to go see for herself. Reluctantly, Señor Ortega agreed to help.

Saturday, January 29, 1763

Señor Ortega has graciously agreed to give us passage to the Americas on one of his supply ships. It is headed for Cape Breton — wherever that is.

It is too early to begin an Atlantic Ocean crossing now. We must wait and begin the voyage in mid-February. It takes two months or more to cross, so that will put us in a North American port in mid-April.

Everything is happening too fast. One day I was

helping Marie-Louise dress for a ball, and the next day I am bound for a distant land. I feel like I'm riding a horse without reins.

Sunday, January 30, 1763

I wouldn't mind staying here in Cádiz. It is a beautiful place of flowers, sun, and sea. It is from here that Christopher Columbus set sail on his second voyage to find a better route to the Orient. Instead, he bumped into the island of Saint Domingue. Another horrible place. Attended Holy Mass today and gave thanks that I am not going there.

Monday, January 31, 1763

We are booked on the *Rosa Blanca* one of Señor Ortega's supply ships. The captain is Gaston. That is it. No name other than Gaston.

Two and a Half Months Later
Friday, April 15, 1763

I'm on the other side of the Atlantic Ocean! Fort Louisbourg, on the island of Cape Breton. The month is spring, but the wind says it is winter!

I have never been this cold in my life. My nose is cold. My ears. My hands. My feet. My teeth are cold. The crossing was hard enough. I stayed sick most of the time, but nothing can compare to this awful cold. The crew doesn't smile anymore. They can't. Their lips are frozen in a permanent pout. Captain Gaston gave Ree and me a skin from a creature called a buffalo. It smells, but at least underneath it we are warmer.

Meanwhile the captain has gone ashore to get permission from the authorities to disembark.

Saturday, April 16, 1763

We are still on the *Rosa Blanca*. Gaston has returned with bad news. "The war between France, England, and Spain is over after seven long years." According to officials, a treaty was signed in Paris in February while we were at sea. Gaston went on to explain, "King

Louis XV has given up Acadia, Cape Breton, the Saint Lawrence River Islands, and New France to the British. All forts along the Great Lakes are now under British control. The Spanish were given all lands west of the Mississippi River as payment for being France's ally. France held on to the Caribbean Sugar Islands."

None of that matters to me. I wonder, will I ever be warm?

"Will they allow us to get off the ship?" Ree asked anxiously.

"The officer in charge, Captain John Woolridge, is demanding that all French must take an oath, swearing to accept British authority and obey British law," Gaston answered. "If you agree, then you can enter and move about freely."

"Ridiculous," Ree scoffed.

"You need to understand. The French have been defeated here," Gaston said, sounding somewhat frustrated.

I listened to them talk, but all I wanted to do was sleep. It was snowing — quiet, soft snow. Suddenly, Gaston shook me awake. "Resist," he said. "The Frost King will wrap you in his blanket of warmth and take you to his winter kingdom."

The snow was swirling and turning in the wind. I

fancied I saw the Frost King lurking in the distance. Was I already dead and just didn't know it yet?

"What other options do I have?" I heard Ree insisting.

Gaston cleared his throat. He shifted from foot to foot. "Come back to Cádiz with me."

"That is not an option."

I wanted to ask, why not? I would have gone back to sunny Spain without hesitation. But Ree was committed to finding Jacques.

Gaston shrugged. "According to the Treaty of Paris, you French have the right to fish off Newfoundland. The islands of Saint Pierre and Miquelon are still French. I could take you there."

My teeth were chattering, I was so cold. Ree rubbed her palms to bring heat to her hands. "No, not there."

Gaston sighed. "What about New Orleans? Or the Caribbean Islands of Guadeloupe, Martinique, or Saint Lucia? They are still under the French flag."

No self-respecting French citizen would dream of living under English rule unless they had no choice. Ree felt she had no choice. Her best option was to swear the oath of allegiance so she could continue her search unhindered.

"Gaston, go tell Captain Woolridge that I accept his offer."

Sunday, April 17, 1763

We finally got off the *Rosa Blanca*. And, at last, I am beginning to thaw out a little. Coming from a place where the sun shines most of the year, this is a dreary hole in the earth, filled with snow and ice. I don't like it.

We were escorted to Captain Woolridge's office. I expected him to be an older man, with a sour disposition. But instead he was young, very handsome for an Englishman, with brown hair and matching eyes.

He offered us chairs. I stood by the fireplace and soaked up the warmth. Ree sat across from the young captain. He seemed nice enough, courteous, not at all arrogant as some Cherries can be. That is a name we call English soldiers because of their red uniforms.

Ree showed Captain Woolridge a letter of introduction from Señor Ortega. "I see you are well connected on the Continent," he said, smiling. "Señor Ortega is a very wealthy man whose holdings are extensive. He is backing your expenses one hundred percent for six months while you — " he paused to look at the letter again to verify — "ah, yes, to find your brother, Lieutenant Jacques Boyer. Señor Ortega must love you very much?"

Ree took the letter and returned it to her clutch. "Señor Ortega and my father were best friends from childhood. He is my godfather."

The captain nodded his head and nervously smiled. "You Catholics take your godfathers and godmothers very seriously."

"Very," Ree answered stiffly. "Don't you Protestants?"

"I intended no offense," he said hastily. Anybody with eyes could see that the captain was more than a little interested in Ree. She was so concerned about the pledge, she was unusually short and snappy with her answers. After signing the necessary paper, the captain offered to escort us to Juan Ortega's dwelling.

"This is the Ortega home," Captain Woolridge said, fumbling with his hands. Then the captain paused, took a deep breath, and blurted out, "Pardon me for being forward, but while you are here . . . do you mind . . . if perhaps I might see you again?"

"I think not," Ree answered curtly. "We will be leaving for Fort Niagara within a day or two."

The captain laughed. "It will be several weeks before the ice melts enough in the Saint Lawrence River for you to travel."

Ree sighed. "More delays."

Ice! Snow! In April. Whoever heard of such?

Later

Juan Ortega is in charge of all the Ortega trading business in the Americas. Ree presented Señor Ortega's letter to him, and he and his wife, Carlita, extended their welcome to Marie-Louise.

During the whole greeting, they never addressed me. Never even looked at me. It was as if I didn't exist. Obviously their welcome did not include a slave.

Gaston had several of his men deliver our luggage to the Ortegas later this evening. "We have made a place for your slave to sleep in the storeroom in the shop," Juan told Ree. "We are putting you in the loft."

"Why can't Zettie stay with me in the loft?" Ree asked.

Carlita was taken aback! "Oh," she said, "that's just not done."

It didn't matter, but I'm glad we aren't staying here long.

More . . .

There was enough light left for me to look around.

The Ortegas' house and shop are connected with a hallway in between and two rooms on either side. Living and sleeping areas make up the family quarters. The trading store and stockroom make up the business. Out back is a storage shed and garden space. Ree sleeps in the loft where Baby Frederico will stay when he is older. For now he sleeps in the crib in his parents' room.

I have made my pallet close to the fireplace chimney, where it is warm and comfortable. It will do until we reach Fort Niagara.

(From this point, Zettie Moreau's diary was written in English, as printed here.)

Monday, April 18, 1763

Since I am in British Territory I will need to improve my English. So I will write my diary in English.

Thursday, April 21, 1763

Now I have another reason not to like this place. Carlita.

Carlita is an attractive woman, but with her dark hair pulled back and tied with a piece of ribbon she appears matronly. And she is most disagreeable.

Carlita asked Ree if I would take care of Baby Frederico while she helped in the store. He is a precious child, and I didn't mind watching him. But I wondered.

"If you want me to help, Señora Carlita, why didn't you ask me?" I said.

Carlita was shocked breathless. "How dare you speak to me in that way." Then turning to Ree she asked, "Do you allow this?"

Suddenly the two of them were discussing me as though I were not in the room.

"She has no fear," said Carlita. "Without fear there is no obedience. And a disobedient slave is useless."

She sounded just like Pierre.

Later, Ree came to the storeroom. "Until we learn more about where we are and how people do things here, I'd like you to be more . . . more . . ." She couldn't find the words, so I helped her.

"More like a slave?"

"Well, yes."

Later

The snow has stopped. In the distance I can make out the faint outline of high hills. I imagine what it would be like to stand on top of one of those hills and look out at the sea.

Friday, April 22, 1763

Sunrise. Beautiful. Quiet. Peaceful. The tiny snow crystals look like jewels glistening in the sunlight. How can land so lovely be so hostile at the same time?

Later the Same Day

Today was the first time the weather allowed me to explore Fort Louisbourg. It is much larger than it appears. Although the English flag flies over the fort, the majority of the people here are some other nationality. Swedes, Germans, Spanish, French, Scots, Danes — all the people of Europe living together at this one place. Indians are here, too. But so far, I am the only black at the fort. I thought there would be many slaves here.

It seems impossible that, a year or so ago, all of these people were fighting one another. Now they come here to trade skins for the goods they need. Business is good for the Ortegas.

Gaston's men are unloading the supplies from the *Rosa Blanca*. There is a lot of work to be done. Ree has asked me to help Señor Ortega in the store.

Saturday, April 23, 1763

I have been folding and stacking blankets on the shelf for hours. There is so much in the storeroom now, there is hardly enough space for me to make my pallet.

Sunday, April 24, 1763

I went to Mass and made my confession. Met Father Bernard, a Jesuit priest whose weather-beaten face is as rugged as it is kind. I like him very much.

On the walk back to the Ortegas' house, Captain Woolridge saw Ree and Carlita. He stumbled while hurrying to greet them.

"Hello, Captain Woolridge," Ree said flatly.

I couldn't believe he was flattered by her frosty greeting. "You remembered my name," he said, gushing.

Captain Woolridge is smitten!

Sunday is a day of rest — even for a slave. I left the others and joined Captain Gaston down at the *Rosa Blanca.* Ribbons of orange sunlight streaked the water. Seagulls squabbled over a fish. Large and small ships, with sails at rest, bobbed on the water like toys. I thought about the *Angeline,* my birth ship, and I wondered what it might have looked like.

Later

I had an interesting conversation with Captain Gaston. "I thought there were many slaves in the Americas," I said. "But I am the only one here."

"Oh, there are thousands of your people in the British colonies along the Atlantic," answered Captain Gaston. "And countless more in the Caribbean. Out here in the wilderness you won't find too many slaves. A trapper has no need for one. As more settlers move in and begin to farm and cities grow, then the need for slaves will increase."

"Have you ever been the captain of a slave ship?" I asked.

"Señor Ortega has several slave ships, but I will not captain them," Gaston said. "Nasty business."

And he crossed himself.

"I was an indentured slave," said Captain Gaston.

I had never heard of indentured servants. Captain Gaston said he owed a debt that he could not pay. To keep from going to debtor's prison, he indentured himself. "I had to work for seven years to pay off my debt. Then I was freed."

There is no time limit on slavery. Once a slave, always a slave, unless your master decides to free you. Thinking of my own life — if I were an indentured servant, then I would be free by now. Almost twice.

Wednesday, April 27, 1763

Captain Woolridge came by for a visit this evening. He was so happy about being received by Ree, he almost forgot to greet anyone else. He stayed a respectable time of about an hour, then he prepared to leave.

"You must come again," Ree said as she saw him to the door.

"Oh, yes! If you say so. Yes, ma'am, I would like that. Very much."

Later, I teased her about liking the captain — just a little.

"Oh, no," she said quickly. "He's an Englishman!"

Saturday, April 30, 1763

The month is almost over, yet it is still winter. The wildflowers outside Aix must be glorious by now. Ree and I would be horseback riding about through the fields, if we were there. Here, snow is still on the ground, and even now it is colder than any day I can remember in Provence.

Ree is anxious to get started on the journey south to Fort Niagara. "I am so worried about Jacques," she said. "Every day I waste waiting, he could be suffering unheard-of horrors among the Indians."

Señor Juan has promised to find a guide who will escort us.

Monday, May 2, 1763

Captain Woolridge has become a regular visitor at the Ortega house. When he is in the presence of Ree, he sees only her.

Early Tuesday, May 3, 1763

I was frightened out of my wits today. While working in the shop alone, the door opened. There stood the most horrifying sight I have ever seen. Surely the gates of Hell had opened and two demons had escaped. I crossed myself and asked the saints to protect me.

The short one with straight black hair and dark piercing eyes stood back and glared at me. The tall one had pale gray eyes the color of a winter sky, a shock of blond hair, and a scar stretching from his left eye down his cheek and stopping just below his left jaw. His head almost touched the ceiling, and draped over his shoulder was a wolf skin. That made him look not only bigger but fierce.

The big one spoke — no, he roared. "Where's that Juan Ortega?"

"I-I-I assure you I don't know, sir," I said, swallowing hard. I would have run, but they were blocking the door.

What a sight to behold. Each wore a breechcloth, leggings, a coarsely spun shirt, and fur-lined shoes. I found out these shoes are called moccasins.

The small one had an assortment of pouches, bags,

and knives hanging around his neck and also from his belt. In his hand was something I have learned was a war club. A red woolen cap and mittens completed the attire of this colorful duet.

Just then Juan and Gaston returned. As soon as the four of them saw one another, there were rounds and rounds of slaps on the back, hugs, shouting, and laughter — the greeting of old friends.

Perhaps, I thought, the two are real men and not demons — I suppose.

Later the Same Day

Señor Juan sent me next door to tell Carlita that there would be two extra people for dinner tonight.

"Oh, no," Carlita said, sighing. Then, turning to me, she asked, "Was he a big man with a booming voice, blond hair, and a scar? And did he have an Indian with him?"

I answered yes.

Carlita's shoulders slumped. "Put away anything that is likely to break," she told Ree. "Armand Dusant is back! He is one of New France's best trappers, and by far one of the kindest souls I know, but he's also very hard on furniture."

Evening of the Same Day

Carlita seems to have taken it upon herself to teach Ree how a slave should be treated — Spanish style. She is quite good at giving orders. I am expected to curtsy, hold my head down, and speak only when I am spoken to. I must call her Madame Ortega — and Ree, Mademoiselle Marie-Louise. The words tumble over my teeth and tongue. Too many sounds. I'll be glad to leave here.

Later

I learned about Armand Dusant by listening to Carlita tell Ree about him. Born in France but raised in New France, his mother and father were Huguenots — French Protestants who were forced to leave their home. His parents died when he was quite young, but he was taken in by the Micmac Indians of Acadia. Carlita shook her head. "I guess that's why he can't help the way he looks and acts. He's more like them than he is like us."

If Carlita didn't like Armand, that made him a little more appealing, I thought.

Carlita said Armand loves the Indian way of life.

Says it is freer, and less restrictive than living back in Europe. "The Indian," said Carlita, "is an Abenaki named Paul Joseph." That's all she said about him.

Carlita ordered me to serve the meal, after which I could eat.

It was all tolerable, because the big man told such interesting stories about his adventures as a trapper. I soon forgot my indignation.

"A bear put this scar across my face," he said, looking especially at Ree. "I thought I had killed it, but I hadn't. So it was the bear and me, one on one. If it had not been for Paul Joseph happening along at that moment, it would have been over for me. The two of us were able to finish off the bear, skin it, and use his hide to cover us during the winter."

Ree was captivated by the big man. She hung on his every word. Captain Woolridge would have given an arm for her to look at him with that much interest, that much admiration. It has nothing to do with one being a Frenchman and the other an Englishman. There is something bold and unpredictable about Armand that makes him interesting.

 *More* . . .

At last the dishes are clean. I am on my pallet in the storeroom. Exhausted. But before going to sleep, I will use just enough candle to write about Paul Joseph. I have never met an Indian before. Carlita is wrong. All Indians are not savages.

When everyone had eaten, Paul Joseph and I were given our dinner to eat in the hallway. This time I didn't mind being separated. It gave me an opportunity to get to know him.

Paul Joseph told me that when he was not yet fifteen years, he was living near the Androscoggin River, north of the Pigwacket Village, in the District of Maine, which is in the Massachusetts Colony, when the French and English began their war. I have no idea where these places are, but they seem important to Paul Joseph, so I made note of them. Perhaps I'll see a map one day that will show me their whereabouts.

Unlike many Indians, the Abenaki didn't support the French or the English, but this didn't stop their villages from being attacked. "My family fled to the village of Saint Francis in the Saint Lawrence

River Valley, where we lived under the protection of the French." A Jesuit priest baptized him and named him Paul Joseph. "Then, in seventeen fifty-nine, Robert Rogers and his Rangers attacked and destroyed Saint Francis. My family was scattered to the four winds. Some members returned to their ancestral homeland. Some became nomadic, roaming from place to place."

Paul Joseph ventured north into Nova Scotia and Cape Breton, where he married a Micmac woman. Then he teamed up with Armand. They became partners in trapping. "I serve as a guide, and Armand provides the gunpowder, which Indians can't acquire from British authorities." The French had been far more open to trading guns and gunpowder to the Indians than the English.

"There is a lot of unrest among the nations. War belts are passed from one to the other. Indians who were friendly to the British and fought on their side are now sorry they did. The French only wanted to hunt and trade. The English want land — Indian land. Things are not settled yet. There will be more fighting."

At the end of the evening, Juan informed Ree that

Armand and Paul Joseph were going to be her guides to Fort Niagara. "We leave on Friday," said Armand, slapping his hand on the arm of the chair he was sitting in. The chair arm fell off, broken in two. Poor Armand gushed apologies, and Carlita pretended not to be upset.

No better news — we will be leaving this place in a few days!

Wednesday, May 4, 1763

All morning I helped Armand and Paul Joseph pack the supplies for our trip to Fort Niagara.

Carlita still talks about me to Ree as if I am not in the room. To her, I am not a person.

"Juan has agreed to let me have a slave. He finally sees how good Zettie is with little Frederico, and how much she helps at the store," she told Ree. "So, I was thinking . . ." she continued slowly, "why don't you let us buy Zettie from you?"

All I could do was stand by and listen.

"Who needs a companion on a journey like the one you are getting ready to take?" Carlita asked.

"She is not for sale," Ree said.

"Then hire her out to me until you return. We will pay you well."

I wasn't a thing! I felt like running, but to where? I felt like screaming, but who would hear? I felt like crying, but who would care?

"Please let me buy her. Think about it."

"How much are you willing to pay?" Ree asked, looking at me for the first time. My heart sank. She was told to name her price. "I don't have a price," said Ree, winking at me. "Zettie is not for sale."

I could breathe again. When we were alone, Ree laughed. "Frightened you, didn't I?"

"No. I knew you wouldn't sell me," I lied. It bothered me that if she did want to sell me she could and there would be nothing I could say about it.

Later

Captain Woolridge came calling this afternoon to tell Ree that he has been reassigned to Fort Niagara. He will serve as the assistant to Sir William Johnson, British Superintendent of Indian Affairs at Fort Niagara. Sir William takes his orders from Sir William Perry, Lord Shelburne, who had been appointed the task of developing policies for dealing with the American territories gained from France. Father Bernard is also going to accompany us on the journey. Good. He has been sent to open a mission in a small settlement south of Fort Niagara on Lake Erie.

So Captain Woolridge and a detail of English soldiers will be traveling to Fort Niagara with Father Bernard and Armand, who are Catholic and Protestant, Marie-Louise, who is French, Paul Joseph, an Indian, and me, an African slave. We have to be in a fantasy land, because this combination of people would never be able to travel together in Europe. It should be an interesting trip.

Friday, May 6, 1763

All our things are loaded on the *Rosa Blanca*. We are ready to depart.

It seems that all I've done for months is say good-bye. I have left the only home I have ever known in France, lived in Spain, traveled across an ocean, stayed at Fort Louisbourg in Cape Breton — and made new friends.

Captain Gaston will transport us to the mouth of the Saint Lawrence River, where we will then load our belongings into small, wooden boats for the river trip.

Saturday, May 7, 1763

We made it to Quebec City and spent the night at the Quebec City Inn. Though tired and still cold, I am able to write. Saying good-bye to Captain Gaston was sad. He had been kind to us.

I was glad to leave the Ortega household, though I will miss Baby Frederico. Carlita was unhappy because Ree would not sell me. But I think it is Carlita's nature to be unhappy.

So far, the river trip has been uneventful. We are traveling on a bateau, a flat boat made of logs held together by ropes.

The English flag shows who governs Quebec City, but most of the inhabitants are still French. Father Bernard said many of the inhabitants — or, as the English call them, settlers — farm tracts of land called seigneuries. Armand added that these are land grants given to noblemen who then rent to settlers.

Sunday, May 8, 1763

As we paddled along the Saint Lawrence River between Quebec and Montreal, the landscape is dotted with whitewashed stone houses. The barns have thatch roofs, and windmills slowly turn in the wind. Occasionally the steeple of a church rises above the trees. It is all very lovely. Very familiar.

Everywhere I look there is wildlife. Abundant. Armand or Paul Joseph pointed out creatures that I've never seen before — otter, beaver, and muskrats. I saw a bear slapping fish onto the bank with its huge paw. I was amazed and terrified at the same time. I thought about how brave Armand and Paul Joseph were, fighting a bear. Its claws could easily rip a person apart.

Monday, May 9, 1763

Today we entered Lake Ontario. It looked like the ocean instead of a lake. We saw Indians fishing in canoes. Armand said they were friendly. We reached Fort Oswego late this evening. Too wet, too cold, and too tired to write more.

Tuesday, May 10, 1763

Left Fort Oswego early this morning. Reached Fort Niagara with daylight to spare.

From what I can see, it is a military fort with a tall

wooden fence surrounding it. We entered over the drawbridge. In the center is a huge drilling field that is surrounded by many different buildings — stables, barracks, a hospital, storage, bake house, and more. Cherries were drilling on the grounds. I saw several cannon, and of course the British flag flying over it all.

We were greeted by Sir William Johnson, who escorted us to a large stone building that is still called by its French name — the *maison à Machicoulis*. Built of dressed stone, it resembles the castles I've seen throughout France. Sir William gave us a brief tour, showing us the first floor where the post offices are located. The second floor has a center reception hall and officers quarters on each side.

Sir William explained that some soldiers have their families with them. Children can stay until age fourteen. Boys have to join the British army or go out on their own. Girls must either marry or return to England.

Ree's room is located on the second-floor corner with a commanding view of the lake. That is the best that can be said about it. In every other way it is plain as bread without jam. A bed. A washstand. A straight-back chair.

Sir William says the third floor of the building is used mostly for storage. My overall impression of the place is not good. It is difficult to find the words in this my second language. But this is a drab building. Somber, stark. Military cold. I am certain that the rooms have a few spirits that lurk about on dark moonless nights. The idea gives me the shivers.

A boy passed us in the hallway. He had a drum slung over his shoulder. He had a likable face with a wide smile, light hair, and dark blue eyes. Sir William called him. "Lemuel, I need you to take Zettie to Lower Town. She's going to be staying in one of the barracks. See Monsieur Clyde Vandermaas. He will show you where."

"Yes, sir," he replied.

Later

"I am Lozette Moreau," I said, introducing myself.

"I'm Lemuel Matthews," he said, pumping my hand like a well handle. "A drummer in His Majesty's army. Are you an African?" he asked matter-of-factly.

I explained that I was indeed an African.

"What does it look like in Africa?" he asked, looking wide-eyed and curious.

I told him I didn't know. I had never been asked about Africa before. It set me to thinking. I could have told him plenty about southern France, but he didn't ask if I was French. He asked if I was African. And I can't tell him one thing about my birth home.

Lemuel told me there were a few blacks at the post — mostly trappers and a slave or two.

Before I knew it, we were in Lower Town. "I have to hurry back for evening duty," he said. But he called over his shoulder, "Maybe we can go fishing sometimes?"

Fishing?

Monsieur Vandermaas was too busy waiting on a customer to show me my quarters. He yelled for a girl named Sally to take care of me. "And hurry right back," he shouted. "You're burning daylight."

"Never mind the Ol' Man," she said. "He's a respector of no one."

I liked Sally instantly. She is English, rather short and round. Two mounds of rosy cheeks rise up on the sides of her pie-shaped face.

By the time we reached the barracks, I had heard Sally's life story. "I was accused of stealing milk," she said. "So I was given the choice of going to jail or becoming an indentured servant for seven years. That's how I came here. The Ol' Man Vandermaas is mean as a hornet and quick to use the stick. I have four more years to go before I will be free of him and his cruelty."

"I am Lozette Moreau," I said. "I am the slave of Marie-Louise Boyer of Aix-en-Provence in southern France. But you can call me Zettie."

"My, my! Aren't you the lady of a lady," she said, smiling. "Well, make yourself at home." She opened the door to a small barracks room. "You're sharing with me."

The space is too tiny to share. Four wide steps and I am across the room. Six big steps and I have gone the length of the room. It has one window and a very small fireplace with one pot hanging on a triangle. There are two pallets on the wooden floor, and one candle and holder. No table. No chair. No washstand. It smells. Insects are swarming. To make matters worse, I have to share it with another person.

More . . .

I didn't see Sally again until late tonight. She was very tired. But when she saw me writing, she became curious. "You can read and write? Saints be praised."

"I am a companion. We are taught well so that we are fit to be in the company of the upper class."

"I've heard tell that the French have strange ideas. No insult intended, but the truth is the truth. I aine never heard tell of a slave mingling with the upper class," Sally said.

"We companions don't mingle with the upper class." I tried to explain the system to the poor girl. "When I accompanied my mistress to the opera, I stood behind her in the shadows in case she needed something. When we went riding, I rode behind her with her friend's companion. And so on. We didn't mingle, as you put it."

"But what else might you be doing as a companion?"

"I don't understand what you mean." I didn't.

Sally clicked her teeth. "Can you milk a cow? Cook? Sew? Wash? Can you do something useful?"

"No. . . ." Sally has rendered me speechless.

Wednesday, May 11, 1763

Sally introduced me to Sam at the woodpile. He is African and a slave of Clyde Vandermaas. "Zettie's a companion," said Sally.

"What's a companion do?" Sam asked.

"Compan," Sally answered, shrugging. We all laughed in good spirit.

In a short while we were talking like old friends. I shared my story from my birth on Captain Moreau's ship to the adventures that had brought me to Fort Niagara.

"You're lucky," said Sally. "Being a companion isn't like being a slave."

"A slave is a slave," I said. "I want to be free."

"All things want to be free," said Sam. "I've seen a creature chew off its leg to free itself from a snare."

I like Sam's and Sally's warm and generous spirits, even though Sally thinks my skills are useless. Sam is quick to laugh, but his eyes show a deep sadness. There is sorrow in him. Deep sorrow.

Sally told me why. "He misses his home in Africa. All he talks about is going back home," she said.

Afternoon

Sally showed me around Lower Town. "We call it the Bottoms," she said. The name fits, because it is located in the lowlands immediately outside the fort.

All around us is a bubbling stew of humanity! From

what I can tell, it seems to be a gathering place for every manner of person who lives. As it was in Cape Breton, people of all nationalities of Europe are congregated in one spot. Boisterous trappers, argumentative traders, discontented Indians, and angry English colonists. Add to that the naying and baying of domestic animals — cows, horses, oxen, chickens, dogs, a few mouser cats, and all varieties of wild critters — that scamper about.

A combination of military and civilian buildings are scattered about. A few structures serve as barracks and storehouses. Civilians have quickly constructed stores. There's an inn of sorts, and several grog shops.

Besides owning Sam and Sally, Clyde Vandermaas owns just about everything. "All he thinks about is money and more money," Sally told me as I walked with her to make a laundry delivery to one of the fort wives.

Vandermaas is also hired by the military to manage the fort wharf and the firewood yard. And he provides a laundry service and a mending service for soldiers who need to get their uniforms repaired. They only get one uniform a year, so it is important to take good care of it.

"I do all the mending," said Sally. "And I help with

the washing. Day in, day out. Sam does anything and everything the Ol' Man tells him to do. Chop wood. Hoe the garden. Tote this. Fetch that. It never ends. And don't make a mistake."

"What will he do?"

"Beat us," said Sally. "You have never been beaten before?"

I remembered Pierre's slap, and my face stung from the memory. "I have been struck once, but never beaten. Ever."

Sally shook her head. "Are you sure you're a slave?" she asked.

"If I decided I wanted to leave here and go beyond the lake, I couldn't go unless I got permission from my mistress. Why? I am a slave."

Sally shrugged, as is her habit. "Why would you want to go beyond the lake?"

I changed the subject.

Evening

After the soldiers are fed, what is then left is fed to the servants and slaves. Sally and Sam supplement their meager diet by fishing, trapping small game, and foraging for berries and wild fruits. We three put our

63

food together, and Sally fixed a dish of bread and beans. It was very tasty.

I like Sam and Sally, and the drummer boy, too. It would have been fun getting to know them better. But in the morning we leave for a place Paul Joseph calls "Boo-fa-loo." It wasn't until Armand pronounced it in French that I understood what Paul Joseph was saying. Beau Fleuve. It means beautiful river. If Jacques is living among the Indians, this will be a good place to get a lead on his whereabouts.

Thursday, May 12, 1763

Last evening Armand stopped by the barracks to bring me a pair of Indian deerskin, thigh-high boots, and a loose overblouse. "These are Mohawk garments," he said, "but I suggest you wear them tomorrow when we travel. The traveling from here is not for petticoats."

I love the feel of the deerskin boots and loose overshirt. The boots mold to the shape of my feet, unlike the wooden shoes I have been wearing. They are softer, lighter than ours, and it is easier to move in them.

My shirt is decorated with beads around the neck and sleeves. I like the way these clothes feel. When we gathered at the river this morning, Ree was dressed as I was. Captain Woolridge, who came along to say good-bye, was horrified. "What is that you are wearing?" he gasped, his eyes stretched wide in disbelief.

"Indian women wear . . ." Armand answered.

"May I remind you that Ree is not an Indian," Captain Woolridge snapped back.

Father Bernard spoke up next. "I must agree that this is not clothing a woman should wear." He shook his head disapprovingly. Then, holding up a finger, he continued. "But . . . it is appropriate for the terrain over which we will be traveling."

Once the good father finished, both Captain Woolridge and Armand had calmed down.

Later

It is sunset. Just enough light left to write. Today I saw the most magnificent sight the Creator has ever created: the Niagara Falls. After leaving Fort Niagara, we journeyed down the river. We left Fort Niagara at sunrise and we are now at Upper Falls. I am exhausted, but I want to write down what I have seen.

Armand rode in the same boat with Ree. She loves the adventure of it all. That seems to please Armand. I can see it in his face. Father Bernard and Paul Joseph and I were in the second boat.

Father Bernard explained that Beau Fleuve is a small settlement of French inhabitants located near Lake Erie on the Niagara River. "Indians have traded at this spot for centuries. Then, when the French came, they established a settlement here in seventeen fifty-eight," Father Bernard explained. "The English burned the settlement during the war, but the inhabitants refuse to leave the land. I am going there to establish a mission."

Jacques's description did not do the scenery justice. The Falls! Majestic. Wonder of Wonders. Beautiful. We heard the roaring water long before we reached it. Plunging water, raging water, mighty water. Falling water.

Paul Joseph explained that the route around the falls was called a portage. The men carried the vessels. Our luggage and supplies were carted by oxen.

The roar of the falls was so loud, we could only

communicate by sign language. Armand led the way. He signaled for us to follow in his footsteps and to be careful. Thank goodness we didn't have on petticoats that would catch in the shrubs along the road.

But the insects are like the plagues of Egypt. On the water, they are not nearly as bad. But on land, the blackflies, gnats, and mosquitoes torment us every step of the way. Paul Joseph plucked leaves from a bush. He indicated for me to rub the leaf on my face, neck, and arms. The leaf repelled the bugs somewhat, but the itching continues.

At the Lower Landing we prepared for the most difficult part of the journey. Awesome cliffs and the great gorge appear as though the earth has a rip in its foundation. On a practical note, the British use this place to transfer goods and supplies. They are in the process of building a cradle that will mechanically take goods up the mountain. They will be finished by next year, I'm told.

The most difficult part of the journey was climbing the rock cliffs to the summit of the escarpment. When our legs could no longer hold us upright, Armand allowed us to stop for a quick meal. Then back on the river and in the boats. "We can reach the settlement before dark if we move out now," he shouted.

Friday, May 13, 1763

We made it to Beau Fleuve, located on the sunrise side of Lake Erie. It is a settlement of crudely built log and stone structures — little more than huts. A lot of living takes place outside. I try not to complain about the bugs and the coldness that touches my bones. Cold mornings are hard to suffer, even though it warms up during the day —

when the sun is out —

which isn't often —

so it is cold —

a lot.

Soon as she arrived, Ree began asking the inhabitants about Jacques. "Did you serve in the French army?" she asked.

"I did."

"Did you know a Jacques Boyer?"

"No."

From person to person. This went on for hours with no positive results.

Later

We are staying with Michel Boudin, a blacksmith, and his wife, Ruth. They seem to be better off than most of the people who live here. They are friends of Armand and Paul Joseph. In France, Paul Joseph, the Boudin family, and Armand could never be friends. But out here in the wilderness they are best friends who genuinely like one another. The warmth among them is sincere.

The Boudins have a lovely baby girl, Phoebe. She is tiny, not much bigger than her pappa's large hands. In a way, the Boudins remind me of the Ortegas at Fort Louisbourg. But the Boudins are more pleasant to be around.

I was glad to help take care of the baby while Ruth and Ree prepared the meal. It is interesting to see how fast Ree is adjusting to the wilderness. She cooked over the fireplace as though she'd been doing it all her life. Yet, I have never known her to pick up a pot before coming here.

Ruth made no demands of me — totally unlike Carlita — just because I was a slave. She talked to me directly and made me feel welcome in her home. The Boudins don't have great wealth or position. Yet they seem very happy. Contented.

Saturday, May 14, 1763

The Boudins are Acadians who don't trust the English. While stuffing ourselves with fresh bread, cheese, boiled eggs, and berries, Michel told us why.

"The place that is now called Nova Scotia was at one time called Acadia. It was our home. We had farms. We had livestock. We had businesses. When the English conquered it, they wanted us to swear an allegiance to their king, but we refused. So the English took our land and forced us to leave. Many of us were transported to Louisiana, or we fled to the New England colonies. But I chose to come out into the wilderness to live among the Indians who are friendly to the French."

"All you've suffered, you seem so happy," I said. "What is the secret of your great joy?"

"We are free here," he said. "Freedom is the source of our happiness."

I mean to be free, too.

Sunday, May 15, 1763

We were awakened this morning by men shouting and dogs barking. A group of about ten or twelve trappers were approaching out of the river fog. "Hello! Hello! We have news!"

Everybody hurried to hear what they had to say. One of the men told us that an Algonquian chief of the Attawa tribe named Pontiac had rallied forces against the British at Fort Detroit. The fort is now under siege.

Pontiac's allies had also attacked and destroyed the British garrison at Fort Sandusky on the shore of Lake Erie. The fighting was fierce.

Later

"It has finally happened," Paul Joseph explained when I asked what was happening. He said a Delaware Indian seer named Neolin had prophesized that if the Indians returned to the ways of their ancestors, they could drive the whites off their land. Neolin also encouraged his people to stop drinking the white man's liquor and wearing his clothing. "Pontiac adopted

Neolin's teachings when the English took over the forts and began treating the Indians harshly," he said.

According to the trappers, Pontiac is heading this way. He is attacking all the forts along the Great Lakes. We must return to the shelter and protection of Fort Niagara.

Some of the inhabitants of Beau Fleuve are refusing to leave. Michel Boudin spoke for those who plan to stay. "We have no quarrel with the Indians. They are angry with the British. Let them fight one another. We will stay neutral."

"The Indians are angry with all whites. They want all of us off their land," someone argued.

Armand tried to reason with his friends. "You don't have to leave forever. Just come to the fort to keep little Phoebe safe." Armand couldn't convince the Boudins to return to the fort. Ree is returning.

Father Bernard said Holy Mass, then announced that he was staying behind as well. For the rest of the day we tried not to worry about what was ahead. The inhabitants put their food together on one table and made a feast for all to share.

I like it here. I wish we could have stayed longer, but I am not altogether sad that we are returning to Fort Niagara. I will get to see Sam and Sally again.

Tuesday, May 17, 1763

We made it back to Fort Niagara. And I am once again in the Bottoms. On my way to see Ree, I saw several girls. I curtsied the way I'd been taught to do. One pushed me. "Out of our way," she hissed at me. "Don't you know your place? You are to step aside when you see us coming."

On my return I saw something else that reminded me of what Paul Joseph had said about unrest among the Indians. There was a line of Indians being waited on by a British officer just outside the gates. The Indians seemed upset. One of them complained bitterly that the lieutenant was not giving him a good deal and that the cost of ammunition was too high.

"When the French were here," the Indian said, "the Senecas had ammunition to hunt, and our goods were paid for with a fair price. Now with the English, the deal is sour. You make enemies of the Seneca who befriended you when you fought the French."

The young lieutenant spoke harshly. "The French lost the war, and so will you if you don't make do with what we give you."

Just then Sir William Johnson interrupted. "You are dismissed, Lieutenant," he said in a firm voice. Then

Sir William calmly addressed the Indian in his language. After the exchange, the Indian shook Sir William's hand and departed smiling. Turning to the young lieutenant, Sir William whispered sternly, "You catch more flies with honey than you do with vinegar."

Later Sally told me that Sir William is married to a Mohawk woman, named Molly. Molly Brant. "The fort wives don't approve. But it aine nothing they can do to stop her from coming to see Sir William. Molly Brant and Paul Joseph are two of only a handful of Indians who are allowed inside the fort."

When I told Sally about what the girls at the fort had done to me, she spat. "Fort girls. Never you mind them. They're a mean lot, especially when you get two or three of them together. They think they are the betters of everybody here in the Bottoms and they love making a scene."

I made a note to avoid fort girls.

Wednesday, May 18, 1763

It rained all day today. I am knee-deep in mud. Cold. And miserable.

Thursday, May 19, 1763

After a rainstorm, Sam can earn a piece of meat or bread by polishing officers' boots with bear grease. While he worked, I got a chance to talk. I asked him how he came to North America.

"It was during a hunt that the hunters became the prey. My peers and I were captured. I alone survived the long journey here. I alone live to tell our story.

"Men came from the trees and began throwing nets over us. We struggled and struggled. We cried for help, but no one came to help us."

The Spaniards chained them together. "I remember we walked for a long, long way to the sea. Then I was put inside a boat with great white wings. In the belly of this flying ship, I could not breathe. I could not see. The other captives cried all night. Some prayed. Some words I understood. They are Benin words. Other words don't make sense to me. I cry and cry. Then I have no more tears. I am thinking death will come soon. I wait. But I don't die. I survive."

Some of the girls I knew in Aix had told me the story of the slave ships, but I never knew one who had actually made the journey. Did my poor mother endure such suffering? "At least you survived," I told Sam. "And you have memory. You know who you are and where you are from."

"I wish I didn't. Maybe it would be easier if I had no memory."

That set me to thinking, and I couldn't go to sleep.

Friday, May 20, 1763

Today, passenger pigeons flew over — thousands of them. There were so many, they darkened the sky. People were batting at them, hurling rocks, shooting bows and arrows — anything to bring them down. Hundreds were killed to be eaten. More were killed for the sport of it. If they kill that many every time, it seems like soon there won't be a flock left.

Sally made a bird stew that was the best I have eaten.

Saturday, May 21, 1763

Monsieur Vandermaas insists that I call him Mister. Behind his back I call him the Ol' Man, same as Sam and Sally. He is always shouting for Sam or Sally to come do this or that. Sam is either fetching water, working in the garden, where all the food is grown for the fort, or delivering laundered clothing. Sally is busy from dawn to dusk, washing or mending uniforms, going to the bakehouse to make deliveries. No wonder in the evenings they are exhausted.

Today, Sam stopped by the barracks and tossed a rabbit in front of the door. "For our meal tonight," he said, and hurried away. What was I supposed to do with a dead creature?

After thinking about it, I decided that cooking a rabbit couldn't be that difficult. So I put it in a pot, added water, and put it over the fire. The fire kept going out, but I finally got it blazing. By the time Sam and Sally came, I had made a grand mess.

They burst out laughing. "No, Zettie," Sally said. "You have to skin the rabbit. Gut it. Wash it. Then boil it!"

We ate cheese and bread and called it a day.

The Ol' Man cornered me today. "What can you do, girl?"

"I attend my mistress, Mademoiselle Marie-Louise Boyer of Aix-en-Provence," I answered courteously.

"Well, if you're gonna stay here, you got to work. You tell your mistress that we don't take care of slaves! Slaves take care of us!"

I hurried to tell Ree what the Ol' Man said. "I'll take care of him," she said. "It's bad enough they keep us separated this way. The officers' wives are such bores," she said. "They talk endlessly about nothing."

Morning, Monday, May 23, 1763

Went to see Ree. Emptied her chamber pot and brushed her hair.

Someone came to her door with a message. Her eyes quickened. She said that Sir William's wife, Madame Molly Brant, was at the fort. Madame Molly has invited several officers' wives to have tea. "I know you want to meet her," she said. "Perhaps you would like to attend with me?" I really wanted to meet Madame Molly, so I gladly accepted.

Later

At the appointed hour I hurried to the castle, dressed in the best of my petticoats, apron, and shawl. Just as I came up the stairs, I overheard two fort wives talking behind me. "No, I'm not going. I'm not interested in socializing with an Indian. That French girl is bad enough, but I hear she's bringing her slave."

"Indeed! We're in the wilderness, but there is no reason to return to barbarity." They laughed.

What they didn't know was that Madame Molly was standing at the top of the steps in the hallway. I quickly took her by the hand and pulled her into Ree's room so she wouldn't have to suffer the humiliation of them knowing she'd heard them.

"I thank you," she said. "What you did was very kind. But I am very accustomed to comments like that. They don't bother me."

Marie-Louise and I spent a wonderful afternoon with Madame Molly. I hope to visit with her again.

Tuesday, May 24, 1763

Ree sent for me. "Look!" she shouted, showing me two dueling swords. "Madame Molly helped me get use of these. We can practice again!"

During our fencing practice, she was more fierce than ever. She disarmed me twice. "You are not concentrating," she said. "Where is your mind?"

The words leaped out of my mouth: "I want to work! I want to be useful."

Ree was shocked. "Work? Doing what?"

"Back in France I asked, would you free me?" She remembered. "Pierre owned me then. But the Toad bought me for you. So it is up to you now. If I can work and take care of myself, will you consider freeing me sooner?"

I had pushed too far. She was angry, I could feel it. "Haven't I been good to you?" Ree shouted angrily. "Haven't I treated you well? Have you ever been hungry? Has being my companion been so awful that all you can think about is being free of me?"

I didn't want to be *free of Marie-Louise.* I wanted to be *free from her.* She didn't understand.

I was quiet. After a while, she sighed. "All right," she said. "You may work if you wish. But you are still my companion. You serve me first. I will make this clear to Vandermaas as well. Now go, Zettie. No more talk about freedom."

Wednesday, May 25, 1763

Sally couldn't understand why in the world I wanted to work. "I'd trade places with you without question," she said.

"I want to be able to take care of myself when I am free," I said.

She took me to see Vandermaas at his shop. I'd rather work for an ogre, but the Ol' Man is the only one hiring.

His place is a lot like the Ortegas' at Fort Louisbourg. The house and business are connected. It is built of stone and horizontal logs slotted into upright posts at regular intervals, with a steeply pitched roof. The entire structure is surrounded by a picket fence. I have seen houses styled like these dotting the countryside throughout Provence.

Inside is a large hallway that runs through the middle of the house from the front door to the back door. Big washing pots are in the yard, where women wash every day. There is a barn for animals — cows, chickens, and pigs — with another fence around that. The English do love their fences.

To the left of the hallway is a large gathering room with eight shuttered windows: two in the front, four along the side, and two in the back. They are covered with animal skins to keep out the bugs and bitter cold.

Everything is done in the large gathering room — cooking in front of a huge fireplace and sewing. Children of his indentured servants and employees play on animal-skin rugs by the fireplace. There are pots and kettles hanging at different heights over the ever-burning fire, where tubs of water are constantly boiling for washing.

"Mr. Vandermaas, my mistress says I can work," I said.

The Ol' Man growled. "It's about time she made you do something around here. What can you do?"

I never argued that it was my idea to work. "I can speak, read, and write in French and Spanish," I said properly.

His beady eyes narrowed to slits. It made him look reptilian. Then he laughed under his breath. "Read and write, huh? This is Fort Niagara! We are in the wilderness of the New York colony miles from civilization. Nature is hostile toward us. The natives are waging war against us. What useful purpose does a reading and writing slave serve here?"

I had to think fast. "I can figure numbers. And I'm honest. And I am willing to learn other things."

"Ummm. There might be something you can do. You can help me with my inventory and record keeping. I'll make arrangements with your mistress. You'll get food for one meal a day, and Sundays off. That's it."

Once he discussed it with Marie-Louise, I was hired out to his services. "Get to work, Zettie," the Ol' Man shouted. "You're burning daylight."

Thursday, May 26, 1763

Armand has gone back to Beau Fleuve in case he is needed to help defend the settlement. Paul Joseph has gone to be with his wife and family in Maine. He will meet Armand here in the fall to go to their winter hunting grounds.

I will miss Paul Joseph. He is so quiet. When he talks, it is because he has something to say. I like that about him very much.

Friday, May, 27, 1763

Sam's right eye was puffy and red today. "You must have been running hard when you ran into that tree," I said, laughing.

He dropped his head and didn't smile. Instantly I knew I'd said something wrong.

"No tree did that," said Sally, sighing. "The Ol' Man beat him for spilling salt."

I was shocked. "You should report him."

"Who will listen to me? He has the law on his side," Sam answered.

"You don't have a Code Noir?" I asked.

Sam shook his head. "What's that?"

I explained that in France the Code Noir — black code — is a legal document that spells out the rights of slaves and the responsibilities of their masters. A slave master is required by French law to feed, clothe, and shelter his slaves decently. Among other things, they cannot beat or abuse their slaves without just cause. "Spilling salt is not a just cause for a beating!"

Sally put her hands on her hips. "There is no such code here. Besides, if the French Code Noir is so great, why are slaves in the Caribbean so mistreated? We all know how awful it is there."

Sally was right. Slavery in the islands is notorious for its cruelty. I was rapidly learning that slavery is a monster with many heads. It doesn't matter if the monster speaks French, English, Dutch, Spanish, or Portuguese: The result is the same.

Sunday, May 29, 1763

No sooner had I started working, the Ol' Man gives us a whole week off. Sam and Sally explained that the Ol' Man is of Dutch ancestry. He celebrates Pinxter — or Pentecost in Dutch — which begins fifty days from Easter. It is a weeklong celebration, marked by rest and feasting.

While we ate a lunch of summer sausage, fresh bread, and cider, Sam shared more stories about his home.

"Benin City is where the great king, the Oba, lives. They tell this story. Once there was an Oba who wanted a new palace that was built from the top down," he said. "But no one could tell him how. Then a wise man stepped forward and said, 'Great King, if such a building is to be constructed, then we must follow tradition and allow you to lay the first stone.' Needless to say, the palace was not built in that way, and the Oba learned not to ask his subjects to do what he himself was not able to do."

What a good story. I would love to go to Benin and see the Oba's palace.

Monday, May 30, 1763

Today I prepared a meal for us. This time I roasted a partridge that Sam had caught.

When the meal was over, we talked more about our past. I showed Sam and Sally my mother's cloth. Sam touched it and studied the design. "It is not a pattern that I know. You must understand that Africa is a very, very big place." He gave the cloth back to me.

"One day I will go to Africa and find out who my people are," I said.

Sam leaned against the frame of the door. The night air was cool, and the room was stuffy. He began to sing. It was a lovely song. "Teach it to us," said Sally. And he did.

"It has been four years since I heard my mother's sweet voice singing to me," said Sam. "Sometimes I hear her melody riding on the breezes, and I imagine her working in her garden and remembering her lost son. I miss her. Oh, to hear my mother's voice again."

Tuesday, May 31, 1763

Whenever the bugle blows, all the soldiers report to the parade ground to hear the news. Today, messengers arrived bringing the dreaded news that Pontiac's army had defeated the English garrisons at Fort Saint Joseph on the twenty-fifth and Fort Miami on the twenty-sixth. Reinforcements and supplies were needed if the other Great Lakes forts were going to withstand an attack.

Without hesitation, Captain Woolridge and the other officers began making preparations to fortify Fort Niagara against attack.

Wednesday, June 1, 1763

Down by the wharf, Sam told us today that he is going to run away. "I want to go home," he said.

Sally looked around to make sure no one was listening. "Yes. Go. I will help you," she said.

"It is too unsafe," I argued. "Wait until later, when things have settled down. What is your plan?"

Sam had no plan. He was just going! He would not listen to reason. "There is another story we tell in Benin," he said. "When we die, wherever we are, our spirits will fly away to our homes. So, one way or the other, I will see the great gates of Benin City again."

I will help Sam run away.

Friday, June 3, 1763

Sam is gone. The Ol' Man doesn't know it yet because Pinxter isn't over. I hope Sam makes it back to tell the great Oba what happened.

Later

Messengers brought news that Pontiac's army has captured Fort Quiatenon. His men are on the move, headed for the forts along the Great Lakes. The forts are falling one by one. Fort Niagara is in a state of ready.

"What will the Indians do to Sam if they capture him?" I asked Sally.

"You don't want to know!"

Sunday, June 5, 1763

I awoke from a dream about Sam. I saw him out there in the wilderness running . . . and running. He has nothing to protect himself with. Sam ran past a big bear with long claws. Sam ran by Indians swinging war clubs. Sam ran into the dark waters of the lake. Sam disappeared. I woke up feeling guilty and frightened. The dream is an omen. I feel I have helped Sam escape — to his death.

Monday, June 6, 1763

The Ol' Man was furious when he learned Sam was gone. He promised to do all manner of terrible things to him when he returned. "He's not going to last out there by himself. He'll be back."

I see very little of Ree lately. I still do chores for her, but not much. Whenever she wants to practice her dueling, she sends for me. Otherwise, she is busy being entertained by Captain Woolridge.

Sally and I had a delivery to make this morning. As we neared the picket fence outside the fort where the Indians come to trade, we heard two Cherries talking about Sir William Johnson. "He's got to make up his mind. Either he's an Indian or an Englishman. He can't be both. It's like burning a candle at both ends."

What do they mean? I wonder.

Wednesday, June 8, 1763

It was posted today on behalf of Lord Shelburne that a decree was issued saying that the Appalachian Mountains are a dividing line between colonial settlements and Indian territory. No new settlements are allowed west of the mountains.

"Let the king enforce it," grumbled some of the British colonists who had come to the fort for protection during the uprising.

"The king is in England. Our homes are here. Some of the richest land on the Continent is located in the Ohio River Valley. Now the king and his men tell us we can't move there."

"If the military would get rid of the Indians, we could settle on the land," said another.

"In all of the conversations I heard today," I told Sally this evening, "nobody said one word about what the Indians wanted."

Has anybody thought that maybe that's why the Indians are so angry?

Thursday, June 9, 1763

Reports of more fighting. And it is getting closer to us. Criticism of Sir William mounts, as his Indian policies are coming under attack here at the fort.

Monday, June 13, 1763

I've been busy. But I took time to make myself a set of pockets today. Sally liked them, so I promised to make her a pair. "They are very handy for carrying things," I said. "You can wear them underneath your petticoat or on top of it."

"The French can be very clever," said Sally. "I wonder why English women didn't think of something like this?"

"I'll make you a set for your birthday. When is that, Sally?"

To my surprise, she didn't know. "I'm an orphan," she said. "Nobody ever told me when I was born."

Everybody has a birthday — the day you were born. So I told Sally to choose any day she would like to be born and that would be her birthday. She thought about it and said, January first.

"What is your last name?" I asked. She'd never been

given one, either. So I told her to choose a name. "I like springtime when the flowers bloom. So I will call myself Sally Bloom," she said.

"How does this sound: Sally Bloom, born on January first?"

Sally cried because she was happy. "I got a name and a birthday. That makes me somebody now."

Tuesday, June 14, 1763

A young man came into the shop today. He asked if I could read. I said yes. He handed me a letter. It was torn and tattered. "I got it some weeks ago, but I can't read it. Would you read it to me?" he asked.

I read the letter from his mother, telling him that his family was well. His little sister, Meg, is marrying Thomas, a young man from a neighboring village. He smiled. "I know the bloke. Nice enough, Thomas is. He'd better be good to her."

When I'd finished, he gave me an egg. Sally and I shared it for our supper.

Wednesday, June 15, 1763

The bugle sounded this morning. New message. Fort Venango and Fort LeBoeuf have fallen to Pontiac.

I wonder about Sam. Where is he? Whatever is happening to him?

Monday, June 20, 1763

All day I helped the Ol' Man count goods and stack them neatly on a shelf. He grumbled and fussed the whole time.

The mosquitoes are particularly bad today. Swarms of them sting my legs.

Tuesday, June 21, 1763

There are always people coming through the Bottoms with word about what's going on in the interior. Several trappers have reported seeing "white men" fighting in Pontiac's army.

"They are probably French," said an English colonist. "They were in league with those devils during the war."

"They could very well be English, Spanish, or

Dutch," said a Swedish trapper. "This country is full of *coureurs des bois*."

The colonist was silenced.

Later, Sally explained that a *coureur des bois* was a trapper or trader — usually French but included any European who knew the patterns of the rivers, the language of the Indians, and their ways of trade and war. They usually married Indian women and had children These children were sometimes called *métis* (mixed). The families of *coureurs des bois* live in their own villages and move freely among European and Indian cultures. "It wouldn't surprise me none if there was plenty of white men fighting with the Indians out there."

Immediately I thought about Jacques. Has he become a *coureur des bois*?

Tuesday, June 28, 1763

Word has spread that I can read. Many of the men in the regular army and some of the men in the colonial militia can't read or write. They pay me small tokens of food or material to write letters or to read letters they have received. The Ol' Man doesn't bother me about it, because it brings business to his shop.

I just read a letter to a young private from England. His sweetheart was tired of waiting and so she wed another. The young man took the news quite well. He shrugged and said, "Thank you, Zettie. No need for me to cross the ocean again then, is there?"

For payment, he gave me a pint of milk.

"This is far better than the stripping," said Sally. That's the last of the milk the cow gives during a milking. It is usually weak and thin. That's what the Ol' Man gives us.

Wednesday, June 29, 1763

Rain, followed by more bugs. I have scratched holes in my arms. I have been wearing the hip-high boots Armand gave us when we traveled around the falls. They protect my legs and they are far more comfortable. I wear my petticoats over them so as not to scandalize the other women.

Thursday, June 30, 1763

The Ol' Man sent us to milk the cows. Sally tried to show me how, but I was nervous and the cow got restless. I fell off the stool and spilled the milk. The Ol'

Man said I was worthless and dared me to go near his cows again.

Rained all night, but cleared by morning. But it remains a cloudy day in my heart. Trappers reported that they had found Sam's body in the Oswego River. Seems he was snakebitten and, with no one to help him, he died.

"Some of the Senecas are siding with Pontiac. You don't know who is or who aine with you," said one of the trappers. "We took time to bury the boy. What was he doing that far away from the fort, anyway?"

"Serves him right," said the Ol' Man, showing no compassion. "He was running away. Serves him right!"

"Seems you're the one lost money on that deal, Vandermaas," said the trapper, showing his disgust. "Far as I'm concerned, that serves you right."

My sentiments exactly!

Sunday, July 3, 1763

Sally and I had our own private ceremony for Sam. The sun was setting on the dark waters of the lake.

We said the Lord's Prayer. I sang the song Sam taught me — the one his mother sang to him. Then Sally took bread and crumbled it into pieces and threw it on the ground. Birds came and ate it. "Now fly away home," she said to the birds. "Take Sam to his beloved Benin." Then we cried.

I seem to always be saying good-bye to somebody. Good-bye in English is just as hard as it is in French.

Monday, July 4, 1763

A detachment of British soldiers reported to the fort today. We later found out that they were led by the famous war hero Colonel Henry Bouquet. Jacques mentioned him in one of his letters. Can't wait to find out more about what's going on.

Tuesday, July 5, 1763

As I rounded the corner of the wharf, I ran right into Colonel Henry Bouquet. He stumbled and almost fell over backward into the water.

"I am so sorry, sir," I said.

Suddenly, the Ol' Man appeared from nowhere and

slapped me. My head jerked around, and the pain made me stumble. I gasped for breath.

"Silly girl," hissed the Ol' Man, who apologized to the colonel, who seemed satisfied that I had been punished.

I wanted to run to Ree, but I didn't. If I were free, I'd have to handle this on my own. So I will.

Wednesday, July 6, 1763

Sally made a paste of pounded oak leaves and rubbed it on my lip. The swelling has gone down.

Another company of men came in today under the leadership of Captain James Dalyell, another war hero.

Whenever there is going to be a big troop movement, I get a lot of requests for letters. Although the soldiers can't be specific about what their orders are, I can read between the lines. Sally gets information, and we put the pieces together.

It seems the English are amassing their forces to fight Pontiac. Dalyell's troops are going west, possibly to relieve Major Henry Gladwin at Fort Detroit.

Thursday, July 7, 1763

Sally and I had an errand at the bakehouse, where all the bread is baked. On the way, we saw Lemuel walking with two fort girls. I waved, because I hadn't seen him since I'd been back. I was glad to see him again. He looked away as if he hadn't seen us.

"I told you fort children don't have anything to do with us in the Bottoms," said Sally.

"But Lemuel isn't like that," I argued.

"No, he's kind and real friendly. But I never speak to him when he's with his fort friends."

Friday, July 8, 1763

Lemuel came by the barracks late this evening to tell us he'd heard about Sam and how sorry he was. "Sam was a nice person."

"Nicer than you," I replied. "How dare you come here. If you can't be our friend in the daylight, then you need not come here in the shadows!"

Saturday, July 9, 1763

Lemuel visited today. "I've got to get right back, but I came to say you was right," he said. "I've decided that my friends are my friends whether in the fort or out of the fort. I will speak wherever I see you, and feel free to speak to me if you're a mind to do so again." Lemuel turned to leave.

"Didn't you promise to take us fishing?" I asked.

"Sure did," he said. "First chance I get off!"

Sunday, July 10, 1763

Something terrible is happening! I overheard the Ol' Man talking with one of Captain Dalyell's assistants. He suggested that Vandermaas give the Indians blankets infected with smallpox. "I agree with Captain Dalyell," said the Ol' Man, "that if every last Indian on the continent was destroyed, it would be a blessing."

The assistant said that Colonel Bouquet doesn't think giving poisoned blankets to Indians was all bad. "I would rather choose the liberty to kill any savage who may come in our way than to be perpetually doubtful whether they are friend or foe," he said.

What an evil plan. The Good Book warns us that we should be careful about the hole we dig for others. We might fall in it ourselves.

If they give disease-infected blankets to the Indians, aren't British soldiers at risk, too?

Thursday, July 14, 1763

It is official. Word has spread around the fort that General Jeffrey Amherst himself has sent a letter to each post suggesting that Indians be given diseased blankets. The fort is divided. I can't believe the number of people who agree with the idea. But not everyone approves. Many of the soldiers don't. Most of the officers do. The colonists do. The trappers don't. Sir William and Captain Woolridge are threatening to resign rather than obey such a terrible order.

Friday, July 15, 1763

Armand is back at Fort Niagara with Michel, Ruth, and Phoebe Boudin and Father Bernard. Armand was able to convince them that they needed to be in a safer place.

It was so good getting to see the Boudins and Baby Phoebe. They have made their camp in the Bottoms, so I get to see them whenever I am not working. Michel Boudin's ability as a blacksmith is needed here, because wagons are in constant use transporting supplies and so are always in need of repairs.

I don't know why, but I feel safer when Armand is around. And one thing for sure, Ree seems happier.

Saturday, July 16, 1763

Steamy. Muggy.

Sally and I spent today gathering in fresh vegetables and storing them in barrels of straw. We have also filled barrels and barrels with water for the wash. Fort Pitt is under siege, so Sir William wants to make sure we are able to endure the siege should we come under attack.

Sunday, August 7, 1763

For weeks, Pontiac's Delaware allies have had Fort Pitt under siege. We have been working night and day helping secure the fort even more than it already is.

To get our minds off war, death, and dying, Sally and I went fishing with Lemuel today. I caught two small fish. Sally caught one, and so did Lemuel. I boasted that I had caught more than they had. "The one who catches the most fish," said Lemuel, "has to clean them — all!"

He was joking, of course. But I learned how to clean fish. Disgusting business, but the result was worth it. We cooked our fish and ate by the lake. A good day. A very good day.

Monday, August 8, 1763

We continue to ready the fort for possible attack. The chances are not likely, but we are getting ready, anyway. The Ol' Man has been screaming all day. "You're burning daylight!"

Whenever I look weary, Sally reminds me, "It was your idea to work instead of companioning!"

Sally knows how to make me laugh.

Tuesday, August 9, 1763

I have used every spare moment writing letters —
one after the other. Soldiers who are fearful that they
may not survive have asked me to pen letters to their
parents, sweethearts, sisters, grandparents. They pour
out their hearts, their real feelings, because they know
I will never tell what they say.

Wednesday, August 10, 1763

We received word that Captain Dalyell's forces were
defeated outside Fort Detroit. That was the official
announcement.

Colonists from farther south come every day, seek-
ing refuge at Fort Niagara. If Fort Pitt falls, Fort
Niagara is next.

Our news is sketchy and unreliable, but we've heard
bits and pieces of information. It seems Captain
Dalyell's surprise attack was betrayed, and Pontiac
dispatched more than four hundred men when they
reached the middle of Parent's Creek. They were ambushed! Refusing to give up his plan, Dalyell charged
ahead and was killed.

Meanwhile, Colonel Bouquet is fighting Pontiac's Delaware allies at Bushy Run near Fort Pitt. Last word, it is going poorly for Bouquet.

Thursday, August 11, 1763

There were cheers when it was reported today that Colonel Bouquet had held at Fort Pitt.

Friday, August 12, 1763

More news about the war. The Delaware have called for peace with the English. Colonel Bouquet's conditions for peace are that all prisoners will be returned and there must be no more fighting. The Delaware have agreed.

Fort Pitt is saved. For the time being, Fort Niagara is not under any immediate threat. But Chief Pontiac continues his siege of Fort Detroit.

Wednesday, August 17, 1763

Visited briefly with Marie-Louise today. She had been out riding with Armand. Word is around that both

Captain Woolridge and Armand are in a pitched battle for her affections. She seems to enjoy both of them.

Lemuel walked with us back to the Bottoms. "Won't get to visit much anymore," he said. Lord Shelburne has been replaced by the Earl of Hillsborough. His visit to Fort Niagara is scheduled for September 2.

Thursday, August 18, 1763

Saints be praised! Jacques has been found!

All this time he has been living among the Delaware. Captain Woolridge brought the news to Ree, who sent for me immediately. She is happy, but concerned.

"When the peace negotiations were taking place with Colonel Bouquet and the Delaware, Jacques served as a translator," she said. She was shaking with emotion. "Once the negotiations were finished, he was immediately put in irons and charged with conspiring with the enemy."

"What will happen to him?" I asked.

"The worst, I suspect," she answered.

I combed her hair and helped her dress for a dinner Captain Woolridge had invited her to attend. She really didn't enjoy being around the fort wives, because they had nothing in common. "I feel like a second thumb on the hand," she said.

Friday, August 19, 1763

The Ol' Man couldn't wait to tell me that my mistress had challenged an Irishman named Robert Sullivan to a duel. "He is one of the best swordsmen in the colony. She doesn't have a chance," he said, laughing wickedly.

But it was my time to chuckle. There wasn't a person on this continent Marie-Louise Boyer couldn't take in a fair duel.

I dressed hurriedly and ran to the castle, taking the flight of steps two at a time.

Captain Woolridge was pacing the floor, insisting that she could not go through with a duel. "You-you-you are a woman, for heaven's sake. You just can't go about dueling with men."

"You English have too many restrictions. Dueling is not just for men," said Ree. She was angry. "Robert Sullivan called my brother a traitor, a coward, and a no-good Frenchman. I demand satisfaction!" Ree would not back down. "Zettie," she said, "you will be my second. We meet at dawn."

"No, Zettie," said Captain Woolridge. "There will be no duel between a man and a woman in this fort."

"Then we will go outside the fort. To the Bottoms. You have no jurisdiction there."

Later

When Armand heard about the duel, he tried to stop it, too. Instead of saying Ree couldn't, he offered to take her place. "Let me defend your family's honor."

"It is not your battle," Ree argued.

When she could not be persuaded otherwise, the duel was set for tomorrow at sunrise.

The whole fort is in an uproar and talking about the duel. Everybody has an opinion. The fort wives think it is disgraceful.

"I think it's exciting," said Sally. "I've never seen a duel before. Your mistress must be powerful good to think she can challenge a man."

"You can't help but admire a woman who has that kind of courage," said Michel Boudin.

Saturday, August 20, 1763

As Ree's second I was up and dressed before the rooster crowed. At dawn, I met Ree at the drawbridge. Mists hovered over the lake. A deer stood silently watching until footsteps frightened it away.

Robert Sullivan and his second were waiting at the designated spot. It was so quiet, we could hear the roar of the Great Falls in the distance.

A group of curious onlookers gathered to see what they hoped would be a good show. Sally, the Ol' Man, the Boudins, the washerwomen, colonists, trappers, militia men.

Captain Woolridge looked even more concerned than the day before. The moment I saw Ree, I knew why. Something was wrong. She was staggering, hardly able to stand upright. Clearly she was sick. I rushed to her. "I am sick to my stomach," she whispered.

"Dry heaves," Captain Woolridge whispered, but not softly enough.

Sullivan and his second suspected something. They took advantage of the moment. "I knew this was all a farce. No woman in her right mind would dare challenge a man," Sullivan said. "She is either addled or just plain foolish." He swaggered around, laughing.

"You . . . Zettie. You . . . please . . ." I understood, and took up her sword.

The crowd roared with laughter. "You can't expect me to fight a slave girl," said Sullivan, enjoying the comedy of it all. "Isn't it against the law?" He laughed.

"If it aine, it ought to be," yelled one of the onlookers. "We can't let slaves go around challenging their betters."

"You know the tradition, Sullivan," Ree said. "I give Lozette Moreau permission to fight in my stead. She is a member of the Boyer household of Aix-en-Provence. By right, she can defend our honor as well as any member of my family can. Meet the challenge or be known as a coward!"

I felt sorry for poor Captain Woolridge. The Bottoms was such an aggravation to his English sensibilities. He was about to dismiss the whole thing as a terrible mistake, until he saw my resolve.

Sullivan wore his arrogance like a coat of armor. Good. Pride goeth before a fall. The smirk on his face turned to a snarl when I engaged him, "On guard."

He had no choice but to defend himself.

I admit, his form was excellent. He is not as skilled as Ree or Saint Georges, but he's good. He attacked, thinking he could overpower me. I countered each move, parried, then thrust. Quickly turned and thrust again. Being smaller, I was able to move faster. I circled around, moving in and out. This threw him off balance. I thanked Saint Georges for showing me how to use my opponent's superior height and weight to my advantage. My strategy was working perfectly.

The crowd wasn't laughing anymore.

Sullivan's second was surprised. "Stop playing and finish this," he said, sounding worried.

Our next exchange began with me attacking. But I immediately stopped and dropped back, leading him to believe I was intimidated. He moved in too quickly. I sidestepped, and when he stabbed past my body, my sword pierced his hand. Blood.

Armand's cheer could be heard above the others. "Touché!"

"I have drawn blood, Monsieur," I said confidently. "Are you ready to admit that you were mistaken when you called Jacques Boyer a traitor, a coward, and a no-good Frenchman?"

Sullivan didn't answer. He allowed rage to manage his thinking, and his moves became amateurish and bullish. With a single move I disarmed him, slinging his sword high into the air. "Grace under pressure." I can still hear Saint Georges telling me that when I had made a good move. "Grace under pressure."

Facing me unarmed, Sullivan had no choice but to apologize to Ree. "I beg the lady's pardon for anything I have said or done that offended you or the Boyer name."

I looked at Ree, who nodded her approval. "Well done, Zettie."

"Satisfied," I responded, bowing graciously to Monsieur Sullivan and saluting him with my sword.

Without another word, he left the Bottoms immediately — I'm told for Quebec.

Without a moment's hesitation, Captain Woolridge rushed Ree back inside the fort to the hospital. Armand followed closely behind.

Michel Boudin lifted me high into the air, cheering. Sally shouted praises. But the Ol' Man looked at me with a different set of eyes. Feeling somewhat naughty, I swished my sword in the air. "I think it is wrong for powerful people to hurt smaller, weaker people — by hitting them and punishing them cruelly. In fact, I don't think anybody should be slapped!"

The Ol' Man rushed inside his shop, looking over his shoulder as if he'd seen a ghost. It made me laugh. Be careful, I told myself. Pride goeth before a fall.

Sunday, August 21, 1763

Ree is very sick. It seems she ate bad food. That is not uncommon around here. Many of our supplies that come through the Falls are tainted. The meat is packed in salt to preserve it. To get around the portage, the carriers sometimes empty the salt to make it easier to carry. Then they pack it with water to give it weight once they reach their destination. The Ol' Man opens barrels all the time that have spoiled. He trades it, anyway. That's probably what happened to Marie-Louise.

Father Bernard came by to pray for her and to scold me for dueling.

Monday, August 22, 1763

Madame Molly came to help. She made a broth and fed it to Ree spoon by spoon. She never left Ree's side. Neither did Captain Woolridge or Armand. "She is fortunate to have two good men concerned about her well-being," said Madame Molly, smiling. "And to have a companion like you, too, Zettie."

As we sat watching Ree, I got a chance to talk with Madame Molly. She is a very interesting woman who has learned how to enjoy both worlds — her husband's and her own. "Don't worry, Little Warrior," she said. "Marie-Louise will be well soon. The sickness will pass. It takes time."

Tuesday, August 23, 1763

Madame Molly was right. Ree was much better when she woke this morning. Sir William visited briefly to see how Ree was feeling. Before leaving, he took me aside. "So, Zettie Moreau, I hear you are quite handy with a sword. I don't approve of women dueling with men. In my wife's culture, if a woman can best a man, then so be it. In this case I will look the other way. Besides, my wife likes you."

I like Madame Molly, too.

Evening

I brought fresh water and a few fresh flowers to Ree, who was sitting up. "Zettie, I've got to go see about Jacques," she said, trying to get out of bed. But she was much too weak to walk.

Then, remembering the duel, she smiled. "You never cease to amaze me, Zettie," she said. "You handled Sullivan well and restored my brother's honor. I didn't know your skills had improved that much. Thank you."

But I had a question. "What was all that talk about the tradition of allowing a slave to defend the honor the same as a family member? I never heard of that before."

Ree smiled. "Nor I, but it was a good bluff!"

Saint Georges would be proud of us!

Tuesday, August 30, 1763

Ree has recovered from her illness. But headstrong as ever, she has convinced Armand to take her to Fort Pitt to see about Jacques. Of course Captain Woolridge did not approve. He wanted to escort her himself, but the Earl of Hillsborough is coming on the second. He has to be here to greet him. The Boudins and Father Bernard are returning as well.

I am staying here at the fort. "I know you can take care of yourself," Ree said, winking.

Thursday, September 1, 1763

They leave at first light this morning. I will especially miss Baby Phoebe. She is a lovable little girl.

The fort has been polished and cleaned for the arrival of the Earl of Hillsborough. The colonists who want to settle the land are hoping that the earl will not follow Sir William's and Lord Shelburne's Indian policies.

Lemuel came to the Bottoms to deliver a message to the Ol' Man. He stayed around until we were finished. We shared a light meal, then talked a bit.

"White colonists want to move into the Ohio River Valley, but Pontiac is blocking the way," Lemuel told us.

I can't help but remember how the soldier had treated the Seneca Indian before Sir William stepped in. "Maybe if the English used a bit more honey, they might be able to make peace with Pontiac."

Friday, September 2, 1763

A runner alerted Sir William that the earl was a few miles away. The whole fort was ready to greet him. Then, to my horror, Pierre Boyer was in the earl's entourage. And he looked right into my face. He was as surprised to see me as I was to see him.

"Saints protect me. Pierre Boyer is at the fort," I told Sally.

"The devil himself must have shown him the way," she said.

What am I going to do? Hide? Run away? None of those are good choices.

"Go see Captain Woolridge," Sally suggested.

I will do so in the morning.

Saturday, September 3, 1763

I tried to speak with Captain Woolridge, but he has been too busy. "Later, Zettie," he said. There may not be a "later" for me.

Sunday, September 4, 1763

Pierre reached the captain first. He went to Captain Woolridge and claimed that I was his slave. I couldn't defend myself against him. He also brought charges against Marie-Louise for possession of stolen property. Captain Woolridge had no choice but to put me in the fort's prison until Marie-Louise returned and the matter could be settled.

Here I am again, waiting to find out what my fate will be. Where will I end up now?

Monday, September 5, 1763

When Sir William Johnson found out I was in the fort's prison, he released me. I am in his custody until the matter can be settled. He sent for me to report to his office in the castle.

"You were kind to my wife, Zettie. I want to help you, but you must tell me the truth," said Sir William.

I began at the beginning and brought him to this day. I told him about Pierre's mismanagement of the Boyer estate; about him forcing Ree to marry Jean-Paul Beloit, the banker; about her ruse to trick him into buying me as a gift for her. I explained in great detail about our escape with the help of a friend; and our travels to Cádiz, across the Atlantic, to Cape Breton, and finally here. He listened to every word. And when I had finished, he leaned back in his chair.

"Remarkable!" Then he leaned forward again, asking, "Did you really leave the men in their underwear in the middle of the road?"

I was reluctant to answer, until I saw the smile forming in his eyes. We both burst out laughing.

Thursday, September 8, 1763

There is a lot of movement at the fort, so I wrote many letters today for the soldiers who are going to be replacements. Fort Detroit is still under siege and they need supplies and reinforcements if they are to hold out against Pontiac. But first the supplies must be taken around the Niagara portage.

Another supply detail left for Fort Schlosser at the Upper Landing this morning.

With all else going on, Lemuel has been transferred to Lieutenant John Campbelle's company. They are taking supplies around the Niagara portage. Then they go on to the besieged Fort Detroit. It is a routine trip. He leaves in a few days. I hope I'll get to see him, but my future is so uncertain.

Friday, September 9, 1763

My hearing was held today.

Marie-Louise does not own me. Pierre does. Even though Jean-Paul Beloit won the bidding, no money had been paid, and no paperwork had been filed. The deal was never finalized before we escaped. Beloit was so angry and embarrassed by the ordeal, he threatened to have Pierre thrown into jail. But Pierre managed to escape to Cádiz as well. That's where he found out where Ree and I had gone.

"If it were up to me, Zettie, I'd free you in a moment. But I don't have the authority to do so," said Sir William. Then, becoming official, he announced, "Lozette Moreau, I release you into the custody of Pierre Boyer, your rightful owner."

Sir William hit the gavel, and the proceedings were concluded.

Pierre grabbed me by my arm and dragged me from the castle. "Where is that sister of mine?" he hissed.

"I don't know," I answered.

"You two really thought you'd gotten away with something," he said. "But I was determined to find you, and I have!"

When I asked him what he was going to do with me, he laughed. "Why, sell you, of course," he answered.

Later

Sally sat up with me most of the night, trying to convince me that everything was going to work out fine. "You always say, 'Look to the hills,' Zettie. Why don't you look to the hills now? You must believe freedom is on the other side."

I am not convinced.

Monday, September 12, 1763

When the soldiers heard what had happened, they decided to buy me. About forty of them donated a coin or two. They took the money to Sir William, who is going to handle all the paperwork and make it legal with Pierre. I will continue to stay here in the Bottoms, hired out to the Ol' Man.

I sincerely appreciate their kindness.

"We couldn't let you be sold away from us," said one of the men. "What would we do without you? You know our secrets. You care about our feelings. You express our ideas with kindness. You never poke fun. You deserve to be free."

Isn't that a twist of fate. Now I'm the property of British soldiers! What next?

Tuesday, September 13, 1763

Lemuel and a few other soldiers left today to meet up with Campbelle's supply company at the Niagara portage. His drum was spit-polished and glittering as he marched past us. "Good-bye," Sally and I called. Lemuel dare not turn his head, but we knew he heard us. "We'll go fishing again when you return."

Later

Pierre caught up with me at the drawbridge. "You don't own me anymore," I said.

"I hear my deserter brother is still alive," he hissed on the "s." "He has ruined my name, pretending to be dead while all along he was living among the savages. If the British don't hang him, then he's facing charges of desertion by French authorities."

Pierre disgusts me. But if he is telling the truth, Jacques is in serious trouble, and no sword in France is good enough to cut it away.

Thursday, September 15, 1763

Sally and I found a broken chair. We cut a tree limb to make a leg and tied it onto the chair. We don't use it to sit on, but as a table.

Friday, September 16, 1763

An attack has taken place at Devil's Hole at Niagara Falls.

We pray Lemuel is safe.

Later

Sally was able to get a few more details about what happened at Devil's Hole. Seems John Stedman, one of the civilian workers, managed to escape and make it to the Upper Landing with the story. A band of Senecas attacked the supply wagons at Bloody Bridge. All the men perished. The supplies and wagons were thrown into the gorge.

What about Lemuel? No one knows anything about Lemuel.

Saturday, September 17, 1763

More bad news. Eight wounded men staggered into Fort Niagara today. They told another grim story. Lieutenant George Sullivan, who was two miles down the river at the Lower Landing of the Niagara portage, heard the gunfire of the first attack at Devil's Hole. He quickly rallied two companies and hurried to assist. But he, too, ran into a trap. Eighty more Englishmen were killed just north of Devil's Hole.

My heart ached for the young men who lay dead at the bottom of the gorge. Was Lemuel one of them? Death, the wages of war. "Maybe Lemuel survived somehow," I said to Sally.

"Not likely," she said. "He'd have to sprout wings and fly out of that gorge."

With all hope gone, we cried ourselves to sleep.

Sunday, September 18, 1763

What does it feel like to be owned by British soldiers? No difference, really. They treat me the same. One of them told me they did it so that Pierre couldn't sell me away from Marie-Louise. They will decide what to do when she gets back.

Slowly the days have become cooler, and the nights are outright cold. Daylight hours are shorter, so the Ol' Man is constantly yelling, "Hurry up, you're burning daylight!"

But he hasn't been nearly as quick to hit me since my duel with Sullivan. He isn't as threatening to Sally, either.

Monday, September 19, 1763

All summer Sally and I have added to our food rations with fresh game. Using bait, a rope, and a box, Sally and I have caught a few things. Today, Sally caught a wild turkey, but when she lifted the box, the turkey fluttered away. It was quite a funny scene watching Sally run around trying to catch a turkey that was trying to fly.

We ate beans tonight and talked about how good that turkey would have tasted.

Tuesday, September 20, 1763

A melancholy hangs over me. I helped Sally mend uniforms all day. My hands are numb. My fingers are sore. Here on my pallet, I hum Sam's mother's song and hold my mother's cloth close. It's difficult to think about Sam and Lemuel without crying.

I look at the trees, which are far in the distance, and they are golden. When did this transformation take place? All this bloodshed, and yet nature defies the ugliness of war by showing herself to be naturally beautiful.

Wednesday, September 21, 1763

Lemuel is alive! Yes, he is. I'm writing it, but it is even now hard to believe.

Sally didn't believe it until she saw him in the flesh. I must admit his story is not easy to accept. As soon as he could, he came to tell us what happened.

During the fighting at Devil's Hole, Lemuel knew he was going to die. Did he jump? Was he pushed? He couldn't remember. Just the falling. "As I hurled through space, the strap of my drum caught on a tree limb and broke my fall. I hung there like a sack of beans for fifteen minutes or more, too stunned and too frightened to move." Then inch by inch he managed to work his way out of the gorge and make his way back to the Upper Landing. From there he came back to Fort Niagara.

Truly, Lemuel is a walking miracle.

Saturday, September 24, 1763

Marie-Louise and Armand are back from Fort Pitt. Captain Woolridge sent for me to come to his office. It reminded me of the day we first met him. He was so official, yet obviously taken with Ree.

Armand insisted upon being present. As soon as she was settled, Captain Woolridge told her about Pierre and the disposition of my case. "Zettie was purchased by the men here at the fort to keep her from being sold away from you," said the captain. Then he added, "Marie-Louise, why didn't you tell me about your brother, the escape, and Beloit before?" He said he had talked Pierre out of pressing charges against her for stealing Zettie.

Ree seemed too weary to speak.

"She has had a difficult time," said Armand, his big voice booming.

She wept softly. "It is all too much," she sobbed.

Armand put his arms around her to ease the sobbing. It did not go unnoticed by Captain Woolridge.

"It's Jacques," Armand whispered. "He's being held as a prisoner of war by the English, but the French have accused him of being a deserter."

Ree could not get any support from Colonel Bouquet. "My brother is going to spend the rest of his days in prison in disgrace. None of what they say is true."

Jacques will be brought here to Fort Niagara in December, where a military tribunal will decide his fate.

Later

Ree begged Captain Woolridge to let me stay with her here in the castle. I could see his resolve melting away. He knew that we needed to talk. And besides, he could deny her nothing.

When we were alone, I told Ree about Pierre and how he found us. "Carlita told him where we were. His intentions were to sell me to Juan and Carlita. But the soldiers bought me instead."

"What will the soldiers do with you?" she asked.

"Who knows?" I answered.

"First, Jacques. Now, you. I can't take any more losses."

Tearfully, she told me about Jacques. He is well. Married to an Indian woman he calls Nancy. "I am the aunt of John, who is two, and Peter, who is a babe in arms," she said, mustering a smile. "They each have Indian names that will take me a while to learn how to pronounce."

Ree said, "At first I didn't know if I could accept Jacques's Indian wife. Until I saw him with his family. He loves them so. And they love him. He is not a traitor, Zettie. He is not a deserter. Nobody will ever make me believe that. He's a wonderful husband and father."

I have a feeling that everything is going to be fine. No reason, I just feel it.

Friday, September 30, 1763

Pierre and Ree exchanged harsh words with each other, and she ordered him out of her life forever. He has left the fort, and we hope we will not see him again anytime soon.

Saturday, October 1, 1763

Raining and cold today. I think about poor Sam buried in the cold, cold ground. Sally reminded me of Sam's story about flying away back to his home when he died. She believes he is back at home in Benin. "I'm sure he has told the great Oba all the stories of his adventures over here," she said.

True or not, it made me feel better. Sally has a way of making me feel better. She's such a good friend.

Later

First snowfall. A light coating. The wind off the lake is heavy. I wrap myself in my mother's cloth, and it warms me enough to sleep.

Monday, October 3, 1763

Since my duel with Robert Sullivan, the Ol' Man asked if I might give fencing demonstrations for guests. I agreed. He's trying to win favor with the fort wives who accept me as entertainment but wouldn't dream of being in my company as a dinner guest. Strange.

Saturday, October 15, 1763

Morning. It was as hot as any summer day and everybody took advantage of the bright, sunny day. Sally and I mended pants and shirts under a tree on the lake side of the fort. We had plenty to do, because at this time of the year, the soldiers' uniforms are tattered and worn. They will be issued new uniforms in January. Then the alterations begin.

More . . .

I wrote a letter for a colonist and he paid with an eel that he'd caught in the lake. I thought at first it was a snake, but when I showed it to Sally, she squealed with delight. "We're going to eat good tonight."

She put it in a pot of water seasoned with parsley. We added a chopped onion, a pinch of salt, and a few peppercorns. The mixture simmered for about an hour, until the eel was tender to the touch. The broth was so tasty.

Sunday, October 16, 1763

It is harder and harder to find late fruits. But Sally and I have managed to put away food for winter. A great eagle circled overhead today. I took that as a good sign. The Indians hold this bird in great esteem. I see why. It is so graceful and majestic.

New supplies came in today, and the Ol' Man worked me long and hard, taking inventory.

Monday, October 17, 1763

The Bottoms will rival anyplace on earth for the unique characters who come through here. I was gathering driftwood down by the river this morning when a man as black as me rowed out of the river fog. I choked back a scream because at first I thought it was the ghost of Sam. But no, the face was far too old.

"They call me Lot Parham," the man said in a deep, commanding voice. "My father named me Abenga Ashun the day I was born. That was in the way back, before the big bird of the waters brought me to this place."

"Pleased to meet you, Monsieur Lot," I said, smiling. I was not just saying it to be polite. I was happy to meet another African. "What place are you from in Africa?" I asked.

"I am from the city of Jenné, on the Niger River. I am of the Soninke people of the Mande speakers. My people have hunted the savannas of the Sahel for centuries."

Niger River. Jenné. Sahel. Savannas. He was speaking another language, yet I was fascinated. I listened to every word Lot said. How his father made a living as a fisherman. And how his mother prepared meals made of yams, peas, and fish. He described the marketplace in his village and the storytellers who taught the children about their ancestors.

Tuesday, October 18, 1763

Sally stood watch so I could talk with Lot without the Ol' Man yelling.

Lot had been the slave of a sailor. He had won a seaman's lottery and bought his freedom. Then he partnered with a French trapper, and together they traveled to Quebec City.

"Tell me about yourself," Lot said. "Where are you from?"

I told him my story.

"Never give up on trying to be free," said Lot. Then he told me a story, one he had learned from his Indian wife. "Wolf was hungry. He came upon Dog, who had plenty to eat and offered to share. Wolf asked him how he was able to live so well. 'You have food. You have warmth.' Dog explained that he served man, and man gave him these things for serving him well. Dog explained that Wolf could also become a servant of Man. But first Wolf would have to give up all his ways. He could not hunt. He could not talk to the moon. He could not dance with the sun. He had to give up his freedom. Wolf decided he did not want to serve Man. 'I may be hungry, but I will remain free,' said Wolf. Which one do you want to be? Wolf? Dog?"

"I am Wolf," I answered. It is my story. One day I will be like Wolf, free to dance with the sun and talk to the moon. But until then I will continue to look to the hills.

Wednesday, October 19, 1763

I almost got into trouble with the Ol' Man today for talking too long. But I am a hard worker, not looking for trouble, so he doesn't bother me too much.

"I grew up wanting to be a blacksmith," Lot said. I

told him about Michel Boudin. "A blacksmith is one of the most respected positions in Mande society. It takes years of hard work, dedication, and discipline to be welcomed into the brotherhood of blacksmiths."

Soldiers come next in Mande society, then there are scholars, craftsmen, merchants, farmers, and then slaves.

"You had slaves?"

"My family did. There was no shame in being a slave. Slavery is as old as time. Among my people, masters sometimes married their slaves or adopted one as a daughter or son. Through such means it was not at all unusual for former slaves to acquire a trade or position of great influence and power. One of our greatest kings was once a slave."

"Now that you are free, why don't you go back to Africa?"

Lot said this was his home now. He had an Indian wife and several children. He had made peace with what had happened to him. "My wife's lifeways and mine are not so different," he said. "We learn from each other."

Later

I am hugging my mother's cloth close. Knowledge fills my head, and happiness embraces my heart. Tomorrow I will show the cloth to Lot. Maybe there is a chance that he will know something about it. Maybe?

Thursday, October 20, 1763

"Allah is merciful," Lot said when I showed him my mother's cloth. "I know this design."

I was beside myself with joy. I told him it belonged to my mother, who was captured. "She died giving birth to me on a slave ship. This is all I know about her. No name. No description."

Lying on our mats, I told Sally what Lot had told me. "The cloth is called a *sudumare*. That means 'the house.' I am from the Peul people, who are also Mande speakers like the Soninke, who are Lot's people. The Mande are like the Iroquois, who are a federation of different tribes that came together for mutual interests. The Mande are not a federation, but they are all kin and share a common language and many customs."

"It makes sense that the motifs on the blanket have

triangles all over it," Lot told me. "These are known as *bitjitgal*, a maternity and fertility symbol representing the female form. This blanket protected your mother from the cold, and also from insects."

For hours I listened to Lot tell me about my people. He taught me a poem my mother would have known. A riddle. Songs. I shared them with Sally. "I am Mande," I told her.

Now I know why Lot Parham looks familiar to me. We have the same prominent nose. The same black skin. The same almond-shaped eyes. The same coarse hair. The same strong arms and legs. We are Mande. I see me in him.

Friday, October 21, 1763

The dark feelings have left me. I felt light as a feather all morning. I think I could fly if I spread my arms. Maybe it is knowing a little about who I am that has helped lift my spirits. Lot left this morning, but I will always be grateful to him for giving me a story. As I close my eyes on another day, I hug my mother's cloth and sing myself to sleep.

Tuesday, October 25, 1763

Another notice was posted today for all to read. I read it for those who needed it. The king of England has taken Lord Shelburne's suggestion, and the Earl of Hillsborough's as well. The king has signed a proclamation that "restricts colonization of whites west of the Appalachian Mountains." But it also requires colonists already settled in those regions to return east.

The Bottoms has been noisy with complaints. The colonists are very upset. Their language is becoming more and more angry. They aren't holding their tongue about their feelings, either.

Wednesday, October 26, 1763

Lemuel stopped by the shop today. He found me stacking things on the shelf. "Where's your companion?" he asked.

"Do you mean Marie-Louise?"

"No," he said. "I mean Sally."

"She's not my companion; she's my friend," I said.

"Companion. Friend. Same thing!"

That set me to thinking.

Thursday, October 27, 1763

Raining. Windy. Colder. Still very busy. The big wash-tubs were emptied and moved inside the shed, where the washing takes place during the winter.

Friday, October 28, 1763

Pontiac has ended the siege of Fort Detroit. Everybody feels relieved. But the fort is still in a state of readiness until the word is official.

I can't stop wondering about what Lemuel said about companion and friend meaning the same thing. As I think about it more, something is becoming clearer and clearer to me.

Tuesday, November 1, 1763

Snowstorm. Swirling snow. Swooshing wind. We did the morning chores, anyway, while the Ol' Man criticized our every move. All Sally and I can do is hug up together and sit by the fire.

Thursday, November 3, 1763

Hog-slaughtering day. I promise never to eat meat again.

Friday, November 4, 1763

The meat had been butchered and divided and hung up to smoke dry. We helped make sausage. The smell of sage makes me sneeze.

My head hurts. Glad to rest. My throat is sore, and I don't feel well. Sally wants to talk, but I don't.

Saturday, November 12, 1763

They tell me I have been ill. The Ol' Man thought I might have smallpox, so he wouldn't let Sally or me come out of our quarters. Sally and Ree nursed me back to health, though, with the help of Madame Molly. I am much better now. Getting better each day.

"You talked in your fever about wanting to fly away to freedom," said Ree. "Does being free mean that much to you?"

"Yes. Oh yes, it does."

Then Ree gave me the news. While I was ill, the

soldiers had sold me to her. "That was always their intention. They knew how much you mean to me. So did Armand. That's why he let me borrow the money." She was so excited. "See, nothing has changed. You are safe. I will never sell you, ever! We can go on with our lives as usual."

My face must have shown my disappointment. I felt more like a thing than ever. How many times had I been bought and sold in the last year?

"Oh, being my companion is not good enough. You want to be free, don't you?" Ree said.

"Please don't begrudge my desire to be free," I said.

"The idea of you not being with me is hard to accept," she said. "You have been a part of my world for most of my life and all of yours."

"Lemuel told me that another word for companion is friend. And it set me to thinking. Do you believe the words mean the same thing?"

"In a way, I guess so," she answered.

"Then why do I have to be a slave for us to be friends? Freedom will not change how I feel about you or Jacques. In a way, it will be better, because I will be choosing to be your friend."

I hope I got her to thinking.

Sunday, November 13, 1763

Feeling much better. Getting my strength back. Sally has been clucking over me like a hen all day.

We've been so busy, I almost forgot Ree's birthday is November 24. She will be nineteen years old — dangerously close to becoming a spinster, yet she never speaks of marriage. I think Captain Woolridge and Armand are getting close to asking for her hand. Which one will she choose? Sally thinks it will be Captain Woolridge. I'm not sure.

Later

I've told Captain Woolridge that Ree is having a birthday on November 24. He is planning a surprise party for her. He said I could come and so could Sally.

I am making Ree a white linen *coif flautant,* a circular cap with two wide streamers that fall down her back. These hats are worn by girls who are over age thirteen and eligible for marriage. I will be eligible to wear one after my birthday in December.

Monday, November 14, 1763

Paul Joseph returned to the fort while I was ill. He and Armand left for the winter hunting grounds at dawn. They had a good day for travel, especially going south. They won't be back until spring. But I think it might be too late for him and Ree by that time. Captain Woolridge is very dedicated.

Tuesday, November 15, 1763

Our hands are stained a reddish brown. We shelled walnuts for the Ol' Man. For each four we shelled for him, Sally and I shelled one for ourselves. "We'll make a fruitcake," she said. "We will have to pilfer the ingrediments one by one from the storeroom," she said.

"Ingredients," I corrected her.

"You know I don't speak French," she said.

I love Sally.

Wednesday, November 16, 1763

Captain Woolridge came to tell me that the officers' wives would not attend Marie-Louise's party if people from the Bottoms, Madame Johnson, or I come. "They don't like the mixing," he said. The hardest part was telling Sally. She had never been to a party before and was so looking forward to it.

Thursday, November 17, 1763

More snow. More cold. I once heard a trapper say that one needed a glass eye, a brass body, and brandy for blood to endure the bitter cold of this land. No sooner do I get used to the terrible blackflies and mosquitoes than winter comes again. There is no escape.

Sally took it well when I told her we were uninvited to Ree's party.

Thursday, November 24, 1763

Ree's party was a surprise. A big surprise. "Where are my friends?" Ree asked Captain Woolridge. He confessed that the fort wives didn't want to mix with blacks, Indians, and people from the Bottoms.

She endured the gathering graciously. But when her guests were gone, she told Captain Woolridge, "Now we have to have another party."

Ree sent Lemuel to fetch Madame Molly, Sally, and

me for another party. When we got the word, Sally was overcome with excitement. "I can't go looking like this," she said. We both looked terrible.

I dug down into my bag and found one of my dresses — one that had belonged to Ree. I gave Sally one of my nice petticoats, and a chemise she could squeeze into. I pulled her hair back and tied it with a piece of ribbon. She looked lovely. When Lemuel saw her, he couldn't close his mouth.

Ree's second party was much livelier than the first, we were told. Someone played the recorder, someone else played the violin, and the dancing began. Madame Molly and Sir William attended, dressed in festive Indian garments, beautifully decorated. They make a striking couple.

Sally's eyes were as bright as stars. "I think I must have died and gone to heaven," she told me as we lay on our pallets. "Thank you, Zettie. Amazing Zettie."

Friday, November 25, 1763

I was writing a letter for one of the soldiers today, when he said something that set me to thinking again. "I guess I could have learned how to read and write, but there was nobody to teach me." A teacher.

Saturday, November 26, 1763

Living here at this military fort has made me soldier-like in my habits. At bugle blast, I rise early, wash my face, say my morning prayers, eat a light meal, then off to work. So goes the rhythm of my days.

Today at midday Sally and I ate a meal of bread, eggs, and cheese. We long for the fresh fruits and berries of summer. Some fruits that have been dried will have to do through the winter.

Monday, November 28, 1763

We practiced our fencing today. I spoke with Ree about her perhaps becoming a teacher. She didn't say no.

Wednesday, December 7, 1763

Ree spoke with Captain Woolridge, who thought it was an excellent idea for Ree to hold classes for the fort children. The fort wives were leery at first, but the children took to learning right away.

Friday, December 9, 1763

I was so busy with my work, I almost forgot that my birthday is today. I am thirteen. Nobody has said a word to me all morning. I think they must have forgotten.

Later

My time to be surprised. Sally came to get me for an emergency. Hurrying to the Ol' Man's shop, I opened the door, and there stood Ree, Captain Woolridge, Lemuel, and many of my soldier friends. "We just want to wish you a very happy birthday," said Ree.

Ree gave me a lovely linen *coif flautant* of my own. "Now that you are thirteen, you can wear one of these," said Ree.

I put it on. I felt so grown up.

Lemuel gave me a smooth rock from the lake. It is so shiny and pretty.

Sally gave me a wooden thimble she had asked the post carpenter to make for me. She paid him with a pot of her good vegetable soup.

"I will treasure my thimble forever," I said.

"It might help you stitch a straight seam," she said, laughing.

Saturday, December 10, 1763

It is warmer than it has been in weeks. Jacques was brought to the fort today. I hear he is being held in the fort prison. His trial is set for the nineteenth.

Sunday, December 18, 1763

I have never seen Ree more worried. She is usually so sure of herself. To tell the truth, I am worried, too.

Monday, December 19, 1763

The military court of three officers convened with Sir William, Colonel Bouquet, and Captain John Freeman. Captain Woolridge felt he was too personally involved to take part in the trial.

They wouldn't let us in, but Sally and I listened outside the door. Lieutenant Jacques Boyer was asked to stand to hear the charges read against him. The most serious one was the crime against His Majesty's forts and conspiring with Indians to overthrow English rule.

I saw him for the first time. He has aged. But he looks strong and rugged. His beard resembles those worn by the trappers I've come to know. Underneath all that tough exterior there is still a quiet and gentle man.

In his own defense, Jacques explained in eloquent form that as a French officer he had been wounded in the head at the Battle of Detroit. When he came out of his coma, four months had passed. He was among the Delaware people.

"Because I knew medicine and how to help the sick, they valued me and kept me well fed. Still, I was their captive. I was allowed to marry, and my wife and I have two sons."

The panel of judges listened carefully to every word Jacques had to say, weighing the evidence for and against him.

Jacques continued. "When Chief Pontiac sent the war belt to the Great Lakes tribes, I tried to use my persuasion to stop the chiefs from waging war."

He said the Indians are angry about what has been happening to their land and the treatment they have received from all whites — French, English, Spanish, no difference. Even now, there is a smallpox epidemic among the Indians. "It is believed that it was given to them in infected blankets. But I cannot believe such an atrocity could be true," he said.

The court stood mute.

Jacques testified that he never lifted a gun or a bow against the English forts that were captured. "On my honor, I never deserted the French army. I fought until I was shot and believed to be dead."

The prosecution could not produce any evidence that Jacques had conspired with the Indians against French forts. No one could testify that they had seen him fire on one British soldier during Pontiac's war.

Colonel Bouquet wanted Jacques to be guilty, but even he could see he had no case. The charges were dropped, and the case dismissed.

The tribunal refused to turn Jacques over to the French. "We have no authority to drop the charges of desertion. May we suggest, however, that you avoid venturing into French territory. This court is adjourned."

Just like that, it was over! Sir William gave us an ugly look when he heard us cheering outside the room. But we were all so happy. Jacques was alive, well, and free. That's what we had hoped for all those months ago when we had set out for this land. It was a good ending.

Sunday, December 25, 1763

Sir William and Madame Johnson have gone among her people on the other side of the mountains. Another good-bye. But I know that I will see them again.

Christ was born on this day. Peace on earth, goodwill to men. It is a starry night. I imagine the sky was full of stars long ago, too.

Monday, December 26, 1763

All day yesterday Ree and I spent talking with Jacques. He told us funny stories about his wife and children. We talked about old times at the house in Aix. He was saddened when he heard about Pierre.

Jacques is anxious to get back to his family. Ree has accepted the fact that her brother will never go home to France. He is a part of this land. His life is here. He leaves in the morning.

Tuesday, December 27, 1763

It was no surprise to me that Captain Woolridge proposed marriage to Ree, but I was shocked when she refused. She has permission to stay at the fort as an employee. She is the new fort teacher.

Later she told me that as much as she admires and respects Captain Woolridge, he is part of the old. Armand is part of the new. "I like the freedom," she said.

I think she finally understands.

Wednesday, December 28, 1763

The Ol' Man is as irritable as ever. Still yelling about daylight. Marie-Louise comes to the Bottoms two times a week and holds classes for the children here. I help when I'm not mending or stacking or fetching. I feel so . . . so . . . useful!

A few of the children can say the alphabet in English and French. In the spring I think I will start a class in fencing. Yes, in the spring. My future seems to be in this place.

Thursday, December 29, 1763

If I am very still, I can hear the roaring waters of the falls. I can see the great eagle circling, and I am filled with awe.

Wrapped in my mother's cloth, I think over the year. When the year of our Lord 1763 began, I was locked in a storage room in Aix-en-Provence, about to be sold. I was miserable. Tonight I am in a room that is no whit larger and is cold most of the time, but I am as happy as I've ever been. Ree told me today that, as of January 1, 1764, I will be a free person. "You deserve to be free, Zettie," she said. "You are loyal and kind, smart and generous. I know that you will be able to make it on your own. My hope is that you will continue to be my friend?"

Saturday, December 31, 1763

Tomorrow is Sally's chosen birthday. I pulled the thread out of an old purse and reused it to embroider the pockets I made for her. Sally's first birthday — her first birthday gift. I couldn't wait to give it to her.

"'Thank you' doesn't seem enough," she said.

"What is given from the heart reaches the heart."
She thanked me, and I knew it was from the heart.

Later

I am Lozette Moreau. All my life I have been told that all English were rude and unkind. That Indians were savages. That Protestants were heretics. And that companions were useless. But I am learning that people are good or bad for many different reasons, but their nationality or station in life has nothing to do with it. We are all human beings.

I know that I am a member of the Mande people of Africa. But I appreciate the part of me that is French; the part Marie-Louise and the Boyers gave me. But I am also Wolf in Lot's story, longing to be free.

That need to be free is a force that draws people to this land. It goes beyond being French, English, Dutch, Spanish, man, woman, rich, poor, slave, or free. I can feel the energy of that yearning all around me in the colonists, the trappers, the soldiers. I feel it in big-hearted Armand, quiet and gentle Paul Joseph, reserved Captain Woolridge, regal Madame Molly and Sir William, knowledgeable Father Bernard, the courageous Boudins, loving Sally, joyful Lemuel, dear,

dear Sam, impetuous Marie-Louise, and even mean Ol'
Man. Theirs is a spirit that cannot be held by earthly
restraints. That same spirit has embraced me. I look,
now, to the hills and I know that on the other side is
tomorrow. Freedom. And I'm almost there.

Epilogue

When she was eighteen, Zettie married an indentured slave by the name of Thomas Adkins. Later she bought his freedom. She stayed at Fort Niagara in the Bottoms throughout the Revolutionary War. She was one of the first black women in the country to earn a military pension.

After the war, the Bottoms were disbanded. Moving to Beau Fleuve, which became the city of Buffalo, Zettie was bitterly disappointed that the newly written United States Constitution did not abolish slavery. The Boudin family, especially Phoebe, remained a part of her life until her death.

Although Zettie had no children of her own, she and Thomas raised several orphans. She became a well-known seamstress in the Buffalo area and was well-known for her designs.

She always hung her mother's blanket on a wall in her house. Although she never got to visit Africa, she made sure that her story was well recorded. When she died, the material was lost. In 1903, her diary, notebook, and cloth were found in the attic of Morris Logan, who said Zettie had raised his grandmother. Mr. Logan gave all the material to the Buffalo Historical Society, where occasionally it is put on display. When she died in 1836, at the age of eighty-six, Zettie was buried with full military honors.

As for the others . . . Inspired by Zettie, Sally decided to look to the hills, too. She moved away to New York City, and she was not heard from afterward.

The Ol' Man relocated to Fort Pitt, which became the city of Pittsburgh, where he opened a dry goods store. Pierre Boyer went to Saint Domingue (Haiti) and managed a sugar plantation there. His cruelty toward slaves was so severe, his reputation was known on three continents. After the Haitian Revolution he escaped to Cuba, where he lived out his life.

Jacques Boyer, his wife, and children moved farther west into Northwest territory. There, he and a mulatto Frenchman named Jean Baptiste Pointe DuSable became good friends and business partners at a place called Eschikago (Chicago).

Paul Joseph fought on the side of the British in the

Revolutionary War and afterward he moved to Quebec. He became a farmer. He and Zettie maintained a life-long friendship.

Armand Dusant and Ree married in the spring of 1764. Captain Woolridge was gracious in his defeat. After the Revolutionary War, Captain Woolridge resigned from the British army. He traveled down the Ohio River to the Mississippi and on to St. Louis, where he helped organize the Louis and Clark expedition that was sent to explore the Louisiana Purchase. He did not travel with the group, but headed back east, where he became the mayor of a small town in Virginia. Zettie read about Captain Woolridge, but there is no correspondence or records to show if they ever met again.

Armand and Ree eventually settled in New Orleans, where they became well-known for their parties. Ree was famous for giving dueling exhibitions, disarming some of the best swordsmen in the colony. It is even rumored that she seriously challenged a New Orleans plantation owner for beating a slave. There is no proof that the duel ever happened. The letters written between Marie-Louise Boyer and Lozette Moreau were the topic of a very popular book published in 1866.

After the Revolutionary War, Lemuel settled near Queenston, a short distance from where he was miraculously saved from a three-hundred-foot plunge into Devil's Hole. He lived until 1821. He and Zettie never visited after leaving Fort Niagara.

Sir William Johnson and Molly Brand remained very much involved with the tribes of the Iroquois Federation and with Indian affairs. When he wasn't living among his wife's people, the Mohawks, he and Molly lived at Johnson Hall in present-day Johnstown, New York. Unfortunately, Sir William died in 1774, at the age of sixty-nine. The Johnsons had eight children, many of whom distinguished themselves in politics, business, and the military. According to records, Zettie corresponded with Molly Brant, whom she always called Madame Molly. Zettie made at least one visit to Johnson Hall.

Although Zettie never heard from Saint Georges, he led a very interesting life. He became world famous for his dueling and was appointed colonel, commanding a battalion composed exclusively of black Frenchmen. They were known as La Légion Saint-Georges.

Chief Pontiac was killed by a Peoria Indian in the vicinity of present-day East Saint Louis, Illinois, in 1769.

When New York did not abolish slavery in its state constitution, Zettie became an outspoken antislavery activist and helped many slaves escape to freedom. Before crossing over into Canada, she always told them: Look to the hills.

Life in America
in 1763

Historical Note

The French and Indian War (1754–1763) was fought between France and England for domination of the vast lands and resources of North America. The war ended on February 10, 1763, when King Louis XV of France signed the Treaty of Paris. The English took control of all previously owned French territory on the continent.

Even though the European powers had made peace with each other, Native Americans became increasingly concerned when white settlements began springing up in the fertile Ohio Valley and Great Lakes areas. The Native Americans resented colonial expansion into their lands, but their anger was fueled by the attitudes of British officers who were managing the forts and trading posts previously run by the French. The rules changed abruptly, and the British stubbornly refused to negotiate fair prices with the Native Americans for trade goods and ammunition. Resentment turned to hostility that finally led to war.

By May 1763, war belts were being passed among the Winnebago, the Miami, the Potawatomi, the Erie, the Huron, and some Seneca tribes. In response to the predictions of a mystic, Pontiac, chief of the Ottawa Indians, attacked Fort Detroit and held it under siege for five months.

Pontiac captured and burned Fort Sandusky on May 17, 1763, Fort Saint Joseph on May 25, Fort Miami on May 27, and Fort Quiatenon on June 1. The British lost Fort Venango, Fort LeBoeuf, and Fort Pitt in June 1763. One of the most devastating defeats for the British came on July 31, 1763, during the Battle of Bloody Ridge just outside Fort Detroit.

In July 1763, General Jeffrey Amherst, commander of the British colonial army, suggested that a way to end Pontiac's Rebellion was to give the Native Americans smallpox-infected blankets. His officers pointed out that British soldiers might also become infected. Others argued that such a plan ran the risk of alienating Native Americans who had once been British allies, such as the Iroquois. Still the plan was implemented and smallpox spread throughout the Native American population, killing thousands of men, women, and children.

Meanwhile, the Delaware tribe held Fort Pitt

(Pittsburgh) under siege, and Pontiac continued his siege of Detroit and made further attacks on other British outposts. From August 2 to 6, 1763, Colonel Henry Bouquet's forces withstood an attack by Pontiac's allies, and on August 10, Bouquet relieved Fort Pitt. He began peace negotiations with the Delaware. Afterward, Pontiac's forces were put on the defense, and his fragile alliances began to fall apart.

George III, who was now king of England, was fearful that other uprisings might happen if "the Indian problem" was not handled wisely. The king appointed Lord Shelburne, and later the Earl of Hillsborough, to develop a policy for dealing with the American territories gained at the Treaty of Paris. He put into place a policy that set the Appalachian Mountains as a dividing line between colonial settlements and Native American lands. The colonists were angered by these restrictions because it halted their plans for expansion of the existing colonies.

King George ignored the complaints of his colonial subjects and signed the Proclamation of 1763 on October 7, which forbade English settlements west of the Appalachian Mountains, and also required colonists who were settled in that region to return east.

Colonists blatantly disregarded the Proclamation of 1763 and settled on Native American lands. The relationship between European settlers and Native Americans further deteriorated, in spite of the efforts of Indian Superintendent Sir William Johnson to stabilize the situation.

After the Treaty of Paris, Sir William Johnson was appointed Superintendent of Indian Affairs in the northern colonies. He was an Irish-born fur trader and land speculator who came to America in the 1730s to manage his uncle's property in the Mohawk Valley of New York Colony. He married a Mohawk woman, Mary (Molly) Brant. During the French and Indian War, Sir William organized and led a group of Mohawk warriors against the French.

Sir William was often criticized because it was felt he associated with Indians too much and took their side too often. Regardless of the criticism he adopted Mohawk dress and practiced many of their customs, which he admired. His Mohawk name was Warraghiyagey, meaning "one who does much or important business." Sir William was trusted; therefore he managed to keep most of the six tribes of the Iroquois Confederacy neutral during Pontiac's uprising.

Sir William was successful in keeping the Iroquois

neutral except for a few Seneca bands, which on September 14, 1763, ambushed a detachment of soldiers at Devil's Hole. Sir William officially reported that five officers and sixty-four privates were killed, in addition to the civilians in charge of the wagons. John Stedman and Lemuel Matthews were survivors.

Lemuel Matthews's story is significant because he was a drummer boy who reportedly was pushed or leaped during the Devil's Hole attack. His strap caught on a projected tree limb and he survived. Lemuel lived the rest of his life in Queenston, New York, not far from the incident. He died in 1821.

The Devil's Hole attack took place on the New York frontier near Fort Niagara, a military fort located at the mouth of the Niagara River, where the discharge of four Great Lakes flows into Lake Ontario. Three nations held Fort Niagara during its long history — France, Great Britain, and the United States.

Outside Fort Niagara was an area known as "the Bottoms." Civilians who worked at the fort lived and conducted business there. Some rough barracks were built to house soldiers as well. British soldiers were allowed to bring their families with them to the fort. But when their children reached age fourteen, the girls were either married or returned to England. Boys were put on their own. Most were inducted into the army or apprenticed to a craftsman.

While the French were the first to penetrate what is now the New York interior by way of the St. Lawrence River and Great Lakes, the Dutch were exploring and settling the eastern side of the New Netherlands Colony as early as 1621. When England gained control of New Netherlands from the Dutch in 1664, they renamed the colony New York. The British became allies and trading partners with the Iroquois. This alliance remained throughout the French and Indian War.

Slaves were involved in the growth and development of the American frontier. The French and Dutch kept slaves, and the British, and later the Americans, continued the system through the Revolutionary War. Most slaves were trained to be skilled craftsmen, house servants, or plantation workers.

It was common among the French trappers, many of whom were adventurous nobles, to have one or two slaves who functioned more as assistants than servants. In the wilds, with dangers at every turn, it was far more practical to have a person at your side who was skilled and trustworthy than a someone whose mind was on freedom.

The Spanish, Dutch, and English were critical of French slavery because of its "peculiarities." For example, there was a caste system among the slaves. The "companion" slaves of the upper class were well educated, well clothed, and well traveled. They were treated differently and taught to believe they were better off than their brethren who did domestic work — cooking, cleaning, and so forth. The domestic slaves thought they were more favored than the field slaves.

The French also developed a legal document called the *Code Noir* (Black Code). It was a series of laws that spelled out the rights and responsibilities of a slave master. Slaves could request assistance from the courts if their masters were guilty of excessive cruelty, starvation, or some other heinous crime against their person.

It was ludicrous to believe that the Black Code could be enforced outside the major French cities. The Code had little effect on the lives of those slaves who worked in the sugarcane fields in the Caribbean. And the slavery practiced in French Haiti was more brutal than anywhere in the world.

Historians mark 1763 as a pivotal year in American history. It was the end of the Colonial Period and the beginning of the American Revolutionary Period. Colonists were growing weary of being governed by a distant king, and the first murmurings of independence were voiced.

A decade later, the Americans were fighting for their independence, this time with the French as their allies.

The French countryside surrounding Aix-en-Provence is marked by rolling hills and rich vegetation.

Chevalier Saint Georges took part in many fencing matches. Above, he is shown competing against a woman.

Slaves captured in Africa were transported on ships to the New World, and often forced to crowd into tiny, filthy quarters. Men and women were usually separated and inhumanely bound by heavy chains.

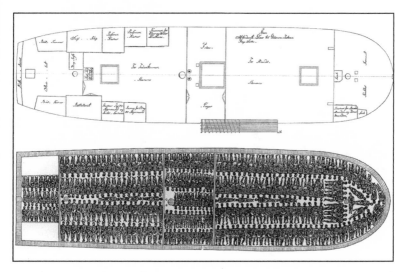

This diagram shows how Africans slaves were to be arranged like cargo on the deck of a ship.

King Louis XIV first secured Cape Breton for France in 1713. He built Louisbourg, a well-fortified, walled city, which became one of the most important and busiest ports in North America. Louisbourg was later attacked and conquered by the English in 1758, but French fishermen and merchants of many nationalities continued to settle there.

Fort Oswego, which was located on the south shore of Lake Ontario, was constructed by the British in 1726, but was captured by the French in 1756 and later reconquered and settled by the English.

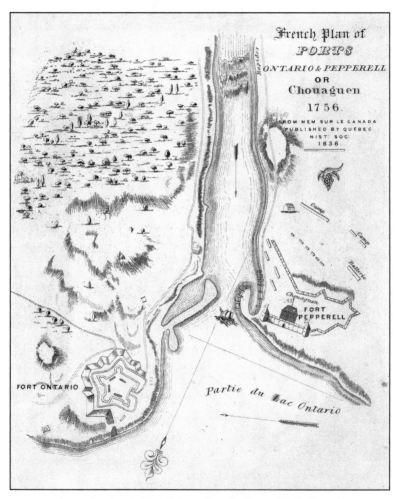

A map showing the French forts along the shores of Lake Ontario.

At the end of the French and Indian War, as they took over forts where the French and Indians had coexisted peacefully, the English began to treat the Indians with contempt and cruelty. In order to drive the British out of North America, Chief Pontiac raised an army from the Potawatomi and Ojibwa nations, along with his own Ottawa people. Pontiac attacked twelve forts in the Great Lakes area, conquered eight of them, and destroyed many settlements. He eventually signed a peace treaty in 1766 and was murdered three years later by an Indian from an enemy tribe.

Fort Detroit, which was originally known as Fort Pontchartrain du Detroit, was built by the French in 1701 and turned over to the British in 1760. A busy trading point for Indians and French fur trappers, Fort Detroit managed to avoid destruction during Pontiac's march. It was the foundation for the modern American city of Detroit.

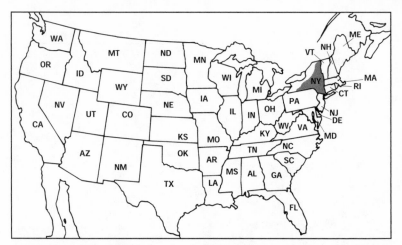

Modern map of the United States, showing the approximate boundaries of New York Colony in the 1760s.

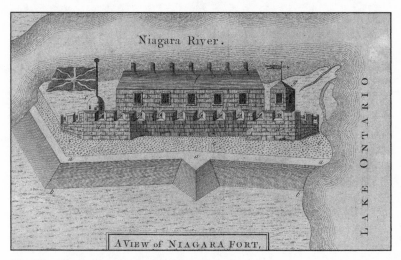

Niagara River.

LAKE ONTARIO

A VIEW of NIAGARA FORT,

Fort Niagara stands at the point where the four Great Lakes pour into Lake Ontario. Whoever controlled Fort Niagara commanded this convergence of waters. For more than three hundred years, France, England, and the United States have struggled in this spot, vying for control of North America.

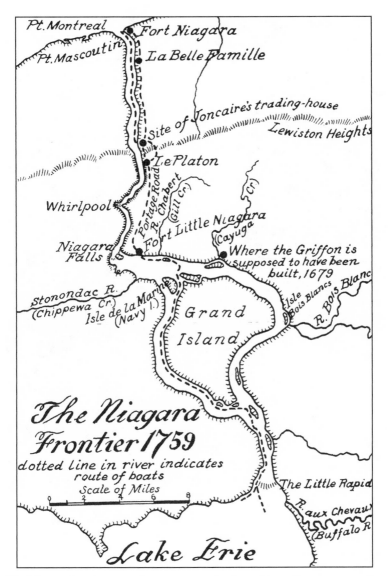

The Niagara frontier was a busy area, overflowing with trading posts as well as military posts.

Sir William Johnson came from Ireland to North America, where he became an important landowner who greatly influenced the settling of the Mohawk Valley. In 1755, Johnson was appointed British Superintendent of Indian Affairs in New York Colony, and his genius in dealing and trading with the Indians had a lasting impact on their relationship with the English.

In February 1763, Sir William Johnson began planning a house that would become the heart of a working estate designed both to encourage settlement and to expand Johnson's control of the land. A mill, a blacksmith shop, an Indian store, barns, and other necessary buildings were added to Johnson Hall, as well as housing for servants.

Molly Brant, a Mohawk, was married to Sir William Johnson in a traditional Mohawk ceremony. Following his death in 1774, she was able to convince the Iroquois Federation to support the English during the American Revolution. At the end of the war, Brant and her children were forced to flee to Canada because of their loyalty to the British. This is why she is featured on this Canadian postage stamp.

About the Author

Patricia C. McKissack, who is the author of several Dear America books, including *A Picture of Freedom* and *Color Me Dark*, enjoys researching history, the cornerstone of this series. The research for this book took her far from her home in St. Louis, Missouri. For example, while visiting Aix-en-Provence, France, McKissack took a tour of the city. She explains. "As our tour guide showed us through several large homes, she explained the French system of 'companions.' These were young girls who grew up as servants of noblemen's daughters. Some companions were indentured. Some were slaves. Some were white and some were Africans or mulattos. By the time I had finished the tour, Zettie and Marie-Louise had taken shape as characters."

Actually, Marie-Louise is based on Emilie de Breteuil, who was a fencing champion. She was good enough to challenge Jacques de Brun, the head of the king's bodyguard, in a public contest. Saint Georges is another fencing champion in French history. "Although I fictionalized the escape in the story, everything else I wrote about him is factual. To learn more about Emilie and Saint Georges, read *Sword* by Richard Cohen," McKissack suggests.

As with most of her work, McKissack relies upon books, personal travel, and contacts with professionals for information on the subject she's writing about. Thanks to Doug DeCroix at Fort Niagara for getting her started on this project, and a special thanks to Susan Dischun, Environmental Education Assistant at the New York State Office of Parks, Recreation and Historic Preservation, who helped her finish. Most of the other information about Fort Niagara comes from *A History and Guide to Old Fort Niagara* by Brian Leigh Dunnigan. As always, McKissack worked closely with her husband and co-author of many books, Fredrick McKissack, whose help was invaluable.

McKissack is an award-winning author who has written more than ninety books for young readers.

"And yes," says McKissack, "the story about Lemuel is true. He did survive the ambush at Devil's Hole."

To the Bookies — Alpine, Alvernyz,
Carmella, Katie, Mary, and Willa

Acknowledgments

Grateful acknowledgment is made for permission to reprint the following:

Cover portrait: *Euphemia Toussaint* (miniature, watercolor on ivory), n.d., 1920–26, by Anthony Meucci, collection of the New-York Historical Society.

Cover Background: *Lake Placid and Adirondack Mountains from Whiteface* (oil on canvas), by James David Smillie, Bridgeman Art Library, No. 155641.

Page 173: Aix-en-Provence countryside, Owen Franken/Corbis.

Page 174: Chevalier Saint Georges, Leonard de Selva/Corbis.

Page 175, top: African slaves on ship deck, Library of Congress, reproduction number LC-USZ62-41678.

Page 175, bottom: Diagram of slave ship, North Wind Picture Archives, Alfred, Maine.

Page 176, top: Louisbourg, researched by the Beaton Library, Nova Scotia; print from the National Archives of Canada, Ottawa, Canada.

Page 176, bottom: View of Oswego, North Wind Picture
Archives, Alfred Maine.

Page 177: French plan of ports, Culver Pictures, New York.

Page 178: Chief Pontiac, SuperStock, Jacksonville, Florida.

Page 179: Fort Detroit, Culver Pictures, New York.

Page 180, top: Map by Heather Saunders.

Page 180, bottom: Fort Niagara, Courtesy of Old Fort Niagara
Association, Inc., Youngstown, New York.

Page 181: Map of the Niagara Frontier, Courtesy of Old Niagara
Association, Inc., Youngstown, New York.

Page 182: *Sir William Johnson*, painting by John Wollaston (working 1736-1767), oil on canvas, c. 1751, Albany Institute
of History & Art, Albany, New York. Gift of Laura
Munsell Tremaine.

Page 183, top: *Johnson Hall*, painting by Edward Lamson Henry
(1841-1919), oil on canvas, Albany Institute of History
& Art, Albany, New York.

Page 183, bottom: Molly Brant postage stamp, Courtesy of the
Canada Post Corporation.

*Other Dear America books
about Colonial America*

The Winter of Red Snow
The Revolutionary War Diary of Abigail Jane Stewart
by Kristiana Gregory

A Journey to the New World
The Diary of Remember Patience Whipple
by Kathyrn Lasky

Standing in the Light
The Captive Diary of Catharine Carey Logan
by Mary Pope Osborne

Love Thy Neighbor
The Tory Diary of Prudence Emerson
by Ann Turner

**While the events described and some of the characters
in this book may be based on actual historical events
and real people, Lozette Moreau is a fictional character,
created by the author, and her diary and its epilogue
are works of fiction.**

Copyright © 2004 by Patricia C. McKissack

Library of Congress Cataloging-in-Publication Data
McKissack, Pat, 1944–
Look to the hills: the diary of Lozette Moreau, a French slave girl / by Patricia C.
McKissack.
p. cm. — (Dear America)
Summary: Brought up in France as the African slave companion of a nobleman's
daughter, thirteen-year-old Zettie records the events of 1763, when she and her mistress
escape to the New World where they are inadvertently drawn into the hostilities of the
ongoing French and Indian War and, eventually, find a new direction in their lives.
ISBN 0-439-21038-0
[1. Slavery — Fiction. 2. Identity — Fiction. 3. African Americans — Fiction. 4. Diaries —
Fiction. 5. United States — History — French and Indian War, 1755–1763 — Fiction.]
I. Title. II. Series.
PZ7.M478693 Lo 2004
[Fic] — 21   2003050435
CIP AC

10 9 8 7 6 5 4 3 2 1   04 05 06 07 08
The display type was set in P22 Cezanne.
The text type was set in Hoefler Text.
Book design by Sarita Kusuma
Photo research by Amla Sanghvi

Printed in the U.S.A   23
First edition, April 2004